A TRUSTING HEART

Jean Morrant

CHIVERS

British Library Cataloguing in Publication Data available

This Large Print edition published by BBC Audiobooks Ltd, Bath, 2008.
Published by arrangement with the Author.

U.K. Hardcover ISBN 978 1 405 64532 4
U.K. Softcover ISBN 978 1 405 64533 1

Printed and bound in Great Britain by
Antony Rowe Ltd., Chippenham, Wiltshire

CHAPTER ONE

With a gasp of relief, Serena turned off the wide promenade into the shade of a small tree-lined square and, setting down her heavy suitcase, fanned herself with her straw hat. Already anxious as to where Clive could be, the oppressive heat now added to her despair. Almost two hours had passed since the time they had agreed to meet—how could he let her down like this?

It was becoming embarrassing, waiting on the pavement, so she decided to move on and take a look at the restaurant her relative owned. And there it was, Bach's Restaurant, across the square, its name on the sun-scorched gold canopy that cast a shadow over the cluster of white-clothed tables and chairs beneath.

It had been Clive who had suggested they meet in Barcelona a day earlier than she was expected. The invitation to spend a little time with him, away from his demanding business life had tempted her, though she had felt more apprehensive about spending the night in the same hotel with him than she had been about meeting her ageing Spanish grandfather, the real reason for her trip.

Well, she wasn't going to wait for Clive any

longer, as her thirst was too great, so she set off across the square and put down her case by the flower pots bordering the cluster of tables. She studied the menu.

The tempting thought of a long, cool drink was foremost in her mind, so much so that she wasn't aware of the soft, running footsteps behind her until she felt a jerk on her arm as her handbag was torn from her grasp and borne swiftly away by a swarthy youth who turned into a nearby alley.

'Hey!' she cried uselessly, quickly gathering her wits. 'Help! Thief! Stop him!' She set off in pursuit, leaving her suitcase behind.

As she ran into the narrow street, hindered by the astonished passers-by, someone overtook her, racing ahead down the crowded alley with the speed of an accomplished athlete. Gasping for breath, she pressed on but soon felt her strength ebbing away. Her legs seemed to turn to jelly and, sapped of all energy, she had to slow her pace. And she had no idea which direction the thief may have taken—he would be well ahead of her by now.

'Damn Clive!' she gasped in frustration as a dreadful thought occurred to her; she had no passport, no money, or any other means of identification.

A Spanish woman came up to her, then another, and both began to chatter excitedly. Soon a small group of onlookers had gathered around her when they learned of what had taken place, their dark eyes gazing upon her in sympathy. On the verge of tears, Serena stared helplessly along the narrow street until, uttering a gasp of astonishment, she spotted the tall athletic figure of the man who had given chase striding towards her, her bag clutched in his hand.

The surrounding group parted and clapped their hands in delight as the stranger drew near. 'Your handbag, senorita?' he queried as he towered arrogantly above her.

'Oh, yes, thank you—I'm so grateful,' she stammered with relief. 'I don't know what I should have done—'

'You should have taken more care!' he broke in harshly, and in perfect English. 'To carry so many items of value is ridiculous!'

'Yes, I realise that, and normally I wouldn't—'

'You tourists will never learn,' he said, interrupting her. 'It gives this city a bad name.'

'Hey, just a minute!' she put in. Although Serena was extremely grateful for the return of her bag, her anger mounted at what she considered an unfair rebuke. 'Anyone would think I was the criminal, not the thief! I have every right to carry with me whatever I wish, and it's not my fault this city harbours criminals. I'm extremely grateful to you, senor, but . . .'

She fell silent as tears of indignation filled her eyes. The stranger's expression softened then and, placing his hand beneath her elbow, he turned to the group of interested onlookers and assured them all was now well with the young foreigner. He escorted her back to the restaurant, where her case was still standing on the pavement.

'Come inside,' he said, picking up her case and indicating the door beyond the tables. 'You appear rather shaken by this episode.'

'Actually, I was about to stop here before this happened so, perhaps, as a small token of gratitude, you will allow me to buy you a drink, or a meal if you wish, though even that would be little reward for your kindness.'

To her dismay, Serena saw a flicker of amusement on his lips. Did he consider her offer an insult, she wondered. After all, he hardly had the appearance of a poor man, quite the reverse, taking into consideration his well-cut, light suit which had the sheen of silk in the fine material, and the gleaming, gold watch-band on his wrist. She tried to compose some sort of apology as he beckoned her to a seat in the corner of the cool, quiet dining-room, but he spoke before she had the opportunity.

'As a matter of fact, I own this place,' he told her with a lift of one dark brow, 'and I think it is you who are in most need of a drink. Perhaps a little brandy.' He signalled the waiter. 'And now, please empty the contents of your bag onto the table.'

For a moment, Serena hesitated before she asked with a certain amount of trepidation, 'Why? What do you want?'

'I want you to check the contents, that's all,' he directed in faintly exasperated tones. 'When the thief realised I was gaining on him, and saw a policeman on duty ahead, he threw down the bag and disappeared up another alleyway. Of course, the bag fell open and most of its contents were on the road, and although I don't think he had time to take anything, I would like you to check. Does my explanation satisfy you?'

'Yes, of course, I'm sorry. I'm still a little shaken.'

'Naturally. Forgive me. This kind of incident happens so often, and the difficulties some tourists experience, well . . .' He gave a despairing shrug. 'They are left without papers—can't speak the language and so are unable to explain their plight to the authorities.'

'Actually, I do speak a little Spanish,' she informed him with a hint of triumph. 'And, thanks to you there doesn't appear to be anything missing,' she added, as she returned everything to her handbag.

'Good! Now, perhaps a glass of brandy will steady your nerves,' he suggested as the waiter reached their table, 'and maybe then you can explain why you were standing in this square with your luggage—and alone?'

She suppressed a gasp of dismay and took a sip of the fiery, amber liquid. How to explain her reason for being here a day early she wasn't sure, yet, by his steady gaze he was impatient for some sort of explanation and, since he had recovered her belongings, she felt she owed him that much. And, if this man was the proprietor, Senor Luis Bachs, he was also the son-in-law of her grandfather. What would Senor Bachs think of her if she told him she had come to meet a male friend. He would surely get the wrong impression of her.

A sudden thought struck her and she glanced through the window. Was Clive now waiting on the street across the square? The impatiently drumming fingers of the man seated opposite caught her attention and she gave him a nervous smile.

'Were you meeting someone?' he asked. And without waiting for her reply, he continued, 'If it was a gentleman, then it was not very wise of him to leave you alone for such a length of time.'

'I haven't been here very long,' she replied. 'I expect he has mistaken the time we arranged or been delayed for some reason.'

'So, it is a gentleman, and you appear to have been standing in the sun for hours.'

She glanced at her watch. 'Well, almost two,' she admitted uncomfortably, 'and, if you will excuse me, I think I should leave. He may be waiting and wondering what has happened to me.'

He smiled. 'I know I would in the circumstances, but I would have been there in the first place.' He ended with a derisive lift of his brow as he rose from the table.

Serena bit back a sharp retort and thanked him once more as she made to leave. What was he going to think of her when she appeared again tomorrow? Perhaps this was the time to explain who she was, right now, but she had to be quick in case Clive was waiting on the main street.

'Senor,' she began as she reached for her case, but his sharply restraining hand on her arm silenced her and she glanced up at him in surprise.

'Leave the case to me,' he directed smoothly, taking it up with ease. 'I shall accompany you to the appointed place just to satisfy myself you are in no further danger.' And he strode ahead to hold open the door.

Outside, as they passed the tables, Serena spotted her pink straw hat under one of them. 'Oh, I'd forgotten all about my hat!' she exclaimed, and he immediately retrieved it. As he handed it over to her she thought, perhaps, his fingers lingered on hers for longer than necessary.

'Now, the only thing missing is your gentleman friend, and let us hope he can be so easily restored to you.'

'Oh, I'm sure there's some simple

7

explanation for his delay,' she said, jumping to Clive's defence. 'Perhaps he missed his plane from Madrid.'

'Madrid?' he scoffed, with a dry laugh. 'There's a flight from Madrid every hour.'

'There may be a strike, or perhaps he couldn't get a taxi from the airport,' she offered, but her heart sank as they reached the corner and there was no sign of Clive.

'There are no strikes today,' he informed her in an infuriatingly calm voice, 'and there is a constant stream of taxis at the airport. Well, do you see your friend?' he asked, his tone faintly mocking as he scanned the pavement.

'No, he doesn't seem to be here,' Serena admitted disappointedly. 'Perhaps he's got tired of waiting and gone to the hotel.'

'I doubt if he is as tired as you,' he remarked with a hint of sarcasm. 'Where are you staying? We can make enquiries.'

Serena felt desperately unhappy, though determined not to let this rather arrogant Spaniard see just how much. She tossed her fair head and said brightly, 'Thank you, Senor Bachs, but there's no need for you to accompany me. If you just direct me to my hotel, I can manage from here. I'm extremely grateful to you but I have no wish to trouble you further.' And giving him the name of the hotel, she reached out to take her case.

'No, no, I can't possibly allow you to go on alone. Your hotel is not too far away. I will leave you there. Incidentally, how did you know my name?

'And tell me something else—you appeared to be observing my restaurant with rather more interest than someone merely finding a suitable place for refreshment.'

Serena shot him a sideways glance but found he was looking straight ahead. His profile, she noticed, was strong—a slightly hooked nose above a determined chin, but his expression told her very little of his thoughts.

'I didn't realise you were watching me,' she said, smiling. 'But I must admit I was looking for your restaurant, though my appointment with you is not until tomorrow. My name is Serena Ferguson—and I am here to visit my grandfather.'

From the corner of her eye, Serena saw his quick glance and turned to face him. His pleasant expression became guarded as he observed her through half-closed eyes before he spoke, his tone lacking the warmth of moments ago.

'So, you are Serena Ferguson from England,' he stated coolly. 'Tell me, why did you not mention this before?'

Serena drew a deep breath. 'There was hardly the opportunity, was there? I mean, we met in very strange circumstances.'

'But had I not asked, would you not have told me?' he queried, his brows rising sharply in his solemn face. And raising a finger to silence her, he added, 'I consider it very strange that you did not mention it before.'

'You are being most unreasonable!' she snapped back, yet she knew he was right; she should have made herself known to him earlier. She experienced a pang of guilt; the anticipated time alone with Clive had caused her to hold back but now the thought of spending it with him had lost some of its glamour.

'I suspect you had a reason,' he returned smartly as he drew to a halt in front of the hotel Estrella and ushered her inside. 'Let us enquire if the gentleman has arrived, shall we? I prefer to ensure you are in good hands before I leave.'

'His name is Clive Mortimer,' she volunteered, knowing he would not leave until he was satisfied all was in order. 'He's just a friend,' she added, uncomfortable under his penetrating gaze.

'Naturally,' he agreed with a mirthless smile. 'Why should I assume otherwise?'

Serena waited beside the desk as he made his enquiries and saw the receptionist shake his head, shooting her a sideways glance. Her heart sank—where could Clive be?

'Your friend has not arrived—in fact, he did not confirm the booking,' Senor Bachs informed her with what she considered a hint of smugness. 'Though I understand a lady made the original reservation by telephone—

10

could that have been you?'

Serena felt colour flood to her cheeks. 'Y-yes,' she admitted uncomfortably, 'I telephoned a week ago and Clive said he would forward the deposit. Are you sure it hasn't arrived?' she asked, directing her attention to the receptionist. 'Maybe it has been overlooked.'

Again, the receptionist shook his head. Most definitely, there had been no confirmation from Senor Mortimer. However, the rooms were available, should she wish to stay. Enveloped by a wave of desolation, Serena turned away from the desk only to meet Luis Bachs' confident gaze.

'As I expected,' he said with an infuriating smile. 'And, as there is now no need for you to stay here, I will telephone your grandfather's house and advise them of your early arrival.'

'Thank you, no.' She declined quickly. 'I will ring Clive's office in Madrid—he must have been delayed.'

'As you wish,' he conceded coolly. 'The receptionist will connect you with the number you require.'

After she had given the name of the company Clive was visiting, the receptionist found the number and made the call. And, as she waited, she prayed there would be a simple explanation for Clive's lateness and so save her dignity in front of this dark Spaniard who appeared to derive some amusement from her

11

predicament.

To her dismay, she learned that Clive had left the previous evening, taking the London flight. And she was horrified when Luis Bachs laid a comforting hand on her shoulder, causing her to swallow hard and fight back the tears.

'Try London,' he advised. 'You have Senor Mortimer's number?'

Serena took her diary from her bag and when, only minutes later, she was connected with Clive's office, it was only to learn that he was attending an important meeting and was not to be disturbed. However, his secretary did agree to ask him to call the hotel as soon as he was free. Biting her lip in annoyance, Serena returned the telephone to its rest.

'So, do I assume you intend staying here?' Luis Bachs enquired, an almost lazy quality to his voice as he lounged against the desk.

'Yes, I prefer to wait until he telephones, but I'll call on you tomorrow as arranged. And thank you again for all your help,' she added, forcing a smile as she extended her hand.

'Until tomorrow,' he said, taking her hand in a lingering grip. 'And hold on to that handbag,' he added as he left the hotel.

*   *   *

After the porter had gone, Serena took a long look around her room; tall windows draped with heavy curtains, a huge, solid wardrobe and matching drawers, and a wide bed with fringed, cotton cover. Her eyes lingered on the bed and she experienced a sickening, hollow feeling inside. In a strange way, she was glad Clive wasn't there. She knew that although she had booked two rooms, Clive had not intended them both to be slept in. She suddenly decided that, even if he did arrive on the evening flight, she would not let him into her room.

'Business before pleasure,' she muttered angrily, recalling his familiar saying, and threw back the lid of her case. How many times had she heard that before? How often had Clive been delayed entertaining an important client, keeping her waiting for hours after she had taken such care with her appearance even though she'd had a hard day on the busy hospital ward she worked on.

Unpacking a change of clothes and her toilet articles, she undressed and took a shower and put on a cool, silk negligee. It was oppressively warm in the room so she closed the shutters against the hot, September sun and stretched out on the comfortable bed to rest. For a while, troubled thoughts prevented sleep, her mind continually invaded by the mocking expression of Luis Bachs as he left the hotel. Somehow, she couldn't erase the picture. Why did she feel so nervous of meeting him the next day. After all, he was only to give her a lift to her grandfather's home in the country, and act as interpreter, for her grandfather spoke no English and Serena had only a smattering of Spanish.

Unable to relax, Serena realised she'd not be content until she had spoken to Clive, and she reached out for the telephone beside the bed. But the call only served to add to her dismay when she learned that he had left the meeting early to drive out of town. Did that mean he had gone to the airport? And, if so, why didn't he ring and let her know?

With a groan of exasperation, she lay back on the bed. If this was the way Clive behaved towards her now, when he professed to love her, what did the future hold? She would have to give it very careful consideration and not allow him to talk her round as he usually did, making her feel guilty for complaining. Juggling with her uncertain thoughts, tiredness eventually overcame her and she fell into a restless sleep.

Serena awoke with a start when the telephone rang, and glancing at her watch realised she'd slept for almost three hours.

'There is a gentleman here to see you, senorita,' the receptionist announced. 'Shall I ask him to wait?'

'Ask him to come up in five minutes,' she replied hastily and, putting down the receiver, rushed to the wardrobe and took out her dress. It was better for them both if she spoke to Clive in the privacy of her room rather than

14

they meet in the crowded lounge downstairs, but she would have to hurry—she'd feel more confident with her hair brushed and a little make-up on her face.

Struggling into her dress, she fastened the row of tiny buttons down the bodice, fumbling in her haste and wondering why she didn't ask to be given more time. Remembering to put back the latch on the door, she slipped on her sandals—she didn't want to open the door to him, she would rather be composed in one of the chairs. It would be much more civilised if they could talk the matter over sensibly.

In the bathroom, she tidied her hair and applied a lipstick, all the time silently rehearsing what she would say to Clive immediately he arrived. Her heart lurched when she heard a tap on the door, but taking a deep breath, composed herself and called for him to enter.

She was just returning the lipstick to her make-up bag when the door opened and, steeling herself, she said with forced lightness, 'Hello, Clive. Now, before you say anything, I think we should have a little discussion about our relationship. You see, I think . . .'

Words froze on her lips as she caught sight of the reflection of the man who was standing in the room. It wasn't Clive, but Senor Bachs who leant casually against the open bedroom door, smiling at her.

She spun round and stared at him,

open-mouthed, taking in his immaculately groomed appearance. 'What are you doing here?' she gasped. 'I wasn't expecting to see you this evening.'

'You did say five minutes, and I clearly heard you invite me in,' he reminded her with a quizzical smile. 'And I must compliment you on making yourself so attractive to receive me.'

'I haven't dressed for your benefit, Senor Bachs,' she returned, her cheeks aflame with embarrassment. 'In fact, I would prefer you to leave.'

'I apologise,' he said with a slight inclination of his dark head. 'I merely came to enquire if your friend had arrived and satisfy myself all was well with you. However, as he has not, perhaps you would care to have dinner with me tonight?'

Serena found she was shaking slightly. It was bad enough being stood up by Clive, but to be reminded of his absence really hurt. She glanced at her watch; if only Clive had had the decency to ring.

'Thank you, but I'd rather stay in the hotel,' she said coldly, crossing the room to open the shutters. 'I'm quite comfortable here.'

'I intended we should eat here, so should there be a call for you it will be more convenient, though I'm afraid it is a little late. If your friend caught the last flight, he would be here by now. We may as well eat in the

16

restaurant.'

'Then I accept,' she said, gathering a little enthusiasm, 'and thank you for your kind thought.'

'Good. That is settled, then.'

As he spoke, his eyes lingered on her, though she couldn't decide if their glittering depths held sympathy for her situation, or mockery. This member of her grandfather's family was curiously different from most men she had encountered, either amongst her colleagues at the hospital, or in Clive's accountancy business.

'You can call me Luis,' he said, and, taking her gently by the shoulders, he kissed her on both cheeks. 'Welcome to Barcelona.'

Surprised by his gesture, she stepped back, gripping the door jamb for support. 'Thank you,' she managed weakly, striving desperately to appear calm. There was something about this man that melted her confidence and she felt strangely vulnerable under his scrutinising gaze. To hide her confusion she moved in to the room on the pretext of finding her bag— anything to avoid those penetrating eyes.

'Don't be embarrassed,' he said softly. 'It is a normal Catalan gesture towards a member of the family, however distant the relationship. And, as one of the family, it is my duty to look to your welfare.'

She spun round to face him, her eyes bright with anger. 'Perhaps you hadn't realised, I am

17

well over the age of consent and quite able to look after my own welfare, thank you, senor!'

'Luis, please,' he prompted, adding mockingly, 'I am relieved to hear my duties will be light—shall we now go down to dinner?'

CHAPTER TWO

During dinner, she was aware of Luis regarding her far more often than she would have expected of someone with whom she had so recently become acquainted. The conversation was general enough—she tried to avoid any subject of a personal nature knowing it may threaten the evening—though, eventually, they ran out of small talk and Serena began to ask about her grandfather.

'I'm going to feel a little strange, meeting him for the first time,' she remarked when the waiter had taken their order.

Luis gave a short, humourless laugh. 'Then how do you imagine his family feel? We didn't know of your existence until after he had called in his solicitor, and it was the priest who broke the news to us less than four weeks ago.'

Serena detected a note of reproach in his tone. 'Until quite recently, I didn't know anything of my grandmother's history,' she responded smartly, 'so I expect our situations are very similar.'

'Hardly,' he said with a touch of rancour. 'I can only thank God his wife is not still alive and has been spared the knowledge.'

'I can well understand how it would have distressed her,' she accepted, seeing the bitterness in his expression. Surely he didn't expect her to take the blame for something quite beyond her control. She flicked him an angry glance, and added, 'I'm sure my family were deeply concerned at the time.'

He leaned forward, his lips curling into a faintly sardonic smile but he was prevented from answering by the arrival of their food.

Whatever else he was, Serena had to admit he was a good judge of her tastes, and she doubted if she could have translated the menu with such pleasing results. Perhaps this could be an enjoyable evening, after all.

'Tell me about your work,' Luis asked pleasantly, almost as though he had guessed a little of the content of her thoughts. 'Do I understand you are in charge of a hospital?'

'Goodness, no!' She corrected him with a laugh. 'I'm senior staff nurse on a children's ward—and I love working there.'

'So, you love children, yet you are not married—a career girl, perhaps?' he asked with a deceptive softness, his dark brows lifting.

'One doesn't have to be married to adore children,' she protested, casting him a reproving glance, 'though I expect the idea of a career would be discouraged in this country.'

He appeared slightly irritated, but said mildly enough, 'My dear young lady, life here is not one long domestic scene as you seem to imagine. This is one of the most progressive areas of Spain and many of our women are in business or have careers—not all consider early marriage as their only goal in life. Naturally, our elders are finding it a little difficult to adjust to the changes in family life and, I must admit, there are times when I am inclined to agree with their views.'

Serena wondered if his wife followed her own profession—could that be the cause of the bitterness she detected in his tone? He hadn't volunteered any information about his wife, and something prevented her from enquiring. It would only serve to boost his ego if she showed interest in his status, though she had to admit, his close regard increased her awareness of him as a man. His dark Latin looks were extremely attractive. She could well understand her grandmother.

'It seems strange my grandfather should suddenly reveal something from the past. I would have thought it a secret he would have wished to take to his grave,' she remarked, collecting her thoughts, and was immediately furious with herself for bringing up the subject again.

However, Luis responded without a hint of animosity. 'Your grandfather, Senor Miguel, has never spoken about the years immediately following the civil war,' he said. 'And I believe he didn't marry until he was over thirty.'

'I understand it was at the end of the civil war when he met my grandmother,' Serena supplied. 'But I wonder why he never asked to see my mother?'

'Initially, I believe that was his intention, but I am sure he will tell you more himself when you meet tomorrow. More wine?' he asked suddenly, and to Serena it seemed he was deliberately changing the subject.

As he called the waiter over, she studied his face, noticing the tiny crinkles near his eyes, and assessed him to be quite a lot older than herself—probably in his mid-thirties, or maybe more—and certainly more mature than Clive. Strangely fascinated, she watched the expressive movement of his lips as he spoke, and the way he ran an expert eye down the wine list until, suddenly, she realised he had returned his attention to her, a flicker of a smile on his sensuous mouth.

'Perhaps something a little sweeter with your dessert,' he suggested, his expression unreadable as he continued to hold her gaze.

'Thank you, I'll leave the choice to you,' she replied, a slightly breathless quality to her voice, 'I'm not used to such a variety.'

He smiled and instructed the waiter to fill her glass. 'You'll soon become more accustomed when you reach your grandfather's vineyard. The grape harvest will begin any day now and the whole household will be involved.'

'Will you be there, Luis?' she asked, more to keep the conversation on its present easy course than because of a genuine interest.

'So, you do not find my company too distasteful, no?' he queried, laughing with a soft mockery at her small sigh of exasperation. 'Yes, you will see me often in the next few weeks. I leave the running of the restaurant to my manager and give assistance with the harvest. You will enjoy it—hard work, but very rewarding. It is an occasion you won't easily forget.'

Serena was quite sure she wouldn't, if these first hours were an example of what was yet to come. She'd been on tenterhooks each moment they were together, though she did find the food and wine had relaxed her mood a little, easing the awful gnawing ache in the pit of her stomach, and Luis could be quite agreeable company when he chose. As the meal progressed, he had refrained from reminding her of her earlier upsets—the incident of the handbag and her fruitless telephone calls to Clive—and now he merely continued to speak of more pleasant matters like the wine harvest, and the celebrations which would follow. Yet, he seemed to think her visit was for far longer than her ticket would allow. Didn't he realise she was here only for three weeks?

'Just a minute!' she put in smilingly, when he spoke of Christmas. 'I'm staying only three weeks; my air-ticket expires on the twenty-ninth. I know my grandfather wishes me to stay for much longer but there are other matters to consider such as my home and . . .' She shrugged, her words trailing off as she thought of the post she'd been offered in the new hospital when it opened.

'So you do not intend to stay here,' Luis wanted to know, 'whatever the outcome of your visit?'

'Naturally, it depends on my grandfather's condition,' she explained, knowing that if the old man was so ill and begged her to stay, her conscience wouldn't allow her to refuse a dying man.

His eyes narrowed speculatively. 'Yes, now I begin to understand,' he said slowly, his arrogant chin thrust forward.

She detected a faint coolness in his tone and, about to remind him she had a living to earn, she supressed the remark; he may get the impression she considered her profession of greater importance than the happiness of an ailing relative. However, he made no further comment and she quickly resumed her attention to the delicious nougat on her plate.

By the time they had finished dessert, the dining-room was crowded, with every table taken. And when Luis rose, suggesting they take coffee in the lounge, she agreed, welcoming the thought of relaxing in an easy chair. But the lounge also was busy, with hardly a vacant seat, and she could barely hear him speak above the babble of voices.

'I asked if you would care for a liqueur,' he

repeated, leaning closer. Then, with an impatient shrug, he reached for her hand, saying, 'It's far too crowded in here, so why don't we have it sent up to your room? I noticed it was adequately furnished and it will be much quieter there.'

For a moment, she hesitated then, feeling it would seem rather ridiculous if she declined, she nodded. After all, however distant the relationship, he was one of the family.

In her room, she took one of the easy chairs when a waiter promptly arrived with coffee and liqueurs which he placed on the low table beside her. As she poured the coffee, Luis took the chair opposite and relaxed, stretching out his long legs as he lit a cigar. Tilting back his head, he released a ring of blue smoke from his well-shaped mouth, watching it thoughtfully as it rose to disperse high in the room. Her eyes lingered on his mouth, strangely fascinated, and only when his lips broke into a smile did she become aware of his regard.

Confused by his dark scrutiny, she looked around her, searching desperately for something to say, and it was with great relief she saw him lean forward and take a bottle from the tray.

'Brandy?' he enquired, pouring a little into two glasses. 'It will help you relax—you've had a very trying day.'

'Perhaps just a sip,' she agreed with a

tremulous smile. 'Too much may make me sleepy.'

'Then a sip it is,' he agreed. 'I don't want you falling asleep, just yet.'

'I think the journey has tired me,' she said, 'though I'm extremely grateful for your company at dinner. I think I would have been nervous on my own.'

Raising his glass, he said, 'Salut! I also have enjoyed dining with you this evening, Serena, and hope you will join me again, very soon.'

'That's very kind of you,' she said, conscious of hot colour rising to her cheeks. And, feeling terribly vulnerable under his penetrating stare, she returned her glass to the table and rose, crossing the wide room to look out of the window.

'I hadn't realised it was so late!' she exclaimed in a rather breathless way, looking up to the darkened starlit sky. 'And yet there are lots of people about.' She babbled on in a voice that sounded unnatural, even to her own ears, the words fading on her lips as she sensed him drawing near.

'The night is young,' he chuckled softly, coming to lean out of the window beside her. 'People will be strolling up and down until the early hours.'

With a soft intake of breath, she edged slightly away from him, the spicy scent of his after-shave lingering in her nostrils. And when again his hand lightly brushed her arm, she gave an involuntary shiver, her awareness of him increasing so that she had to turn back into the room.

'Perhaps I should draw the curtains and put on the light,' she suggested unsteadily, realising as she turned and saw the intimate setting, lit only by the soft glow from one small lamp, that the atmosphere of the room was much too evocative.

For the first few seconds, she was rigid against him, but as his warm lips moved over hers in a slow and infinitely tantalising way, the tension within her subsided. In its place, a breathtakingly new sensation was spreading through her whole body, transporting her to another world when the street sounds floating in on the sultry air faded into the distance. Her heartbeat quickened as he pressed her closer to his lean muscular body, his lips leaving hers to drift down to the soft contours of her throat. She was tinglingly aware of his hand sliding up her spine, coming to rest at the nape of her neck in a soothing caress, causing a tiny moan of delight to escape her parted lips.

'There's no need for you to feel lonely tonight,' he murmured against her ear. Again, he sought her lips.

This time, he kissed her with a hungry insistence, bruising the soft flesh of her mouth. The spell was broken, gone was the comfort and security of his gentle embrace.

'Please,' she protested breathlessly,

struggling against the demands of his lips. 'I think this has gone far enough.'

'Relax, Serena,' he coaxed softly, retaining his hold on her. 'Let us enjoy this time together.'

'I can't,' she cried, wildly seeking to escape his hard embrace. Surely, he wasn't intending to force her to submit?

'Let me go! You're hurting me!'

'Serena, you don't mean that,' he murmured, squeezing her even closer to him.

'I do! Let me go, or I shall send for the manager. Get out.'

She reached for the telephone but, before she could lift the receiver, Luis's hand shot out, his long fingers curling round her wrist. She stared at him, hate and anger burning in her eyes.

To her extreme relief, he released his grip and gave an apologetic shrug. 'Forgive me,' he murmured, 'I wouldn't wish to harm you.' And, with an easy grace, he moved over to the door.

Turning back to face her, his hand resting on the door handle, he gave a thin smile, and said, 'Quite frankly, I am not used to being rejected—by anyone.' And his dark eyes held a threat as he added smoothly, 'But I can wait.' And with a slight inclination of his head, he said, 'Until tomorrow, senorita. Good night.'

As the door closed behind him, Serena let out a shuddering breath and went to drop the latch. As she sat down on the edge of the bed, she uttered a soft moan, aware she was trembling. Yes, it had been foolish to agree to coffee in her room, she ought to have known better.

Rising from the bed, she took a sip of brandy, hoping it would quell the restless ache within. Pacing the room to ease her tension, she caught a glimpse of her reflection in the mirror, noticing immediately how pale she looked in the dim light. Her eyes were wide and dark as she lifted a trembling hand to her lips, now swollen and bruised from his kiss. Then, quickly turning away to blot out the vision, she determined to put the incident to the back of her mind.

But, even after she had climbed into bed, tired as she was, the matter of Luis Bachs continued to invade her thoughts. To her shame, it was the memory of his lips on hers that troubled her, and the feel of his lean, hard body that lingered, and not the indignation she knew she ought to feel.

The following morning, Serena rose early, even though her night had been a restless one. Her disappointment over Clive's failure to put in an appearance and the fact that he hadn't bothered to telephone, had been replaced by an aching bitterness. She was deeply hurt yet, today, found it easier to resist contacting him at his London office, however much she would have welcomed the opportunity to give him a piece of her mind.

With a despondent sigh, she stepped out of the shower and started to dress. This morning, she was enveloped by a terrible feeling of loneliness which, usually, she could shake off in the routine of a busy hospital. But today, she couldn't use work as an antidote for loneliness—she was alone.

Five years before, she had started her nurse training, and soon after that her father had left home, leaving her to comfort her mother who had fretted dreadfully. And by the time she had completed her three year course, her mother had become seriously ill, dependent on Serena for everything. After that, most of her off-duty time had been given to caring for her sick mother, and there had been no spare time for boyfriends. Shortly after her mother died, Clive had come into Serena's life when he became involved in sorting out the family finances. On reflection, they had required very little of his professional services but, from that first meeting with him in his office, they had drifted into a friendship and gradually they became a couple.

She took a grip on herself. It was useless going over it all again and again. Then, just as she finished dressing, the telephone rang and, convinced it would be Clive, she allowed it to continue while she decided on her response. Should she sound cheerful and forgiving, or vent her fury on him for letting her down?

The impatient ringing finally drove her across the room, and picking up the receiver, she lowered herself unsteadily to the bed.

Strangely, she experienced a sense of relief to hear it wasn't Clive on the line—it was Luis Bachs. His greeting caused her a sudden and unaccountable glow of pleasure, until the memories of the evening before came flooding back.

'I was in the shower,' she said coolly. 'I wasn't expecting you to ring.'

'I thought you were avoiding me,' he said with equal coolness, 'though I understand your friend has not yet arrived.'

Again, she grew tense and remarked icily, 'As you have already enquired, there's no point in discussing the matter. And if that was the sole reason for your call, the conversation is closed!' And she returned the receiver to its rest with a firm hand.

She swore under her breath as she stared at the silent telephone beside her. Why must Luis keep reminding her? Anyone would think he enjoyed upsetting her.

A knock on the door interrupted her agitation and she quickly went to open it, to let the waiter bring in her breakfast. But, to her astonishment, Luis was also there. Taking the large tray from the puzzled waiter, he stepped into the room, using his foot to close the door behind him.

'Well, you either had a shower with your

clothes on, or you dress extremely quickly,' he said to her as he set down the tray.

'I didn't realise you'd called from downstairs!' she cried, flushed with indignation. 'If I had known, I wouldn't have answered.'

'I suspect you didn't answer it immediately because you thought it was someone else,' he challenged and, advancing towards her, added confidently, 'Frankly, you sounded quite relieved when you realised I was on the line. So why the cool welcome?'

'Because I don't like being questioned,' she shot back furiously. 'Particularly about my personal affairs.'

'Affairs!' he interjected harshly. And with a cruel twist of his mouth, he added: 'Or the lack of one? I had assumed you would be grateful to have someone to turn to in a situation like this. Apparently, your man friend doesn't care about your well-being or he would have been here.'

'Stop it—please, stop it!' she cried, her voice shaking with emotion as she covered her face. 'Just go away.'

Strong hands took her by the shoulders and she felt herself being drawn helplessly towards him.

'Serena, you little fool,' he murmured and his hand slid up through her hair, resting her head against his shoulder in a comforting caress. 'I don't mean to hurt you,' he continued soothingly, 'but last night you didn't appear particularly heart-broken by his non-appearance—do you love him very much?'

Wordlessly, she shook her head. She wasn't sure any more if she did love Clive, but it was the blunt manner in which Luis had pointed out his shortcomings that had driven all her pent-up emotions to the surface. He must think her a complete idiot, loving a man who didn't appear to return the feeling.

'I'm sorry.' She gulped, avoiding his eyes. 'You must think I'm really stupid.'

'Of course I don't,' he dismissed softly, his long, warm fingers smoothing her tear-stained cheek. Then, as he thrust her firmly away from him, he added meaningfully, 'I'm a patient man—providing it's only sympathy you want.'

With a puzzled frown she moved away from him. 'I'm not sure what you mean.'

A smile of sheer cynicism edged his mouth. 'You're not?' he rasped, his eyes glittering dangerously. 'I'm not made of wood, Serena, so don't play games with me!' And, as though making a supreme effort to shake off some deep emotion, he moved over to the table and lifted the white linen napkin from the tray, and suggested in a controlled voice, 'Perhaps we should have breakfast before the coffee gets cold.'

'We?' she croaked, her nerves jangling as she sank into the chair opposite.

He shot her an impatient glance as he

indicated the tray on the table between them. 'As you hadn't already had breakfast, I decided to join you so that we can discuss our plans whilst we eat. I'm free this morning so I thought you might like a look around the city before we drive to your grandfather's house this afternoon.'

Stunned, Serena could only stare at him until, managing a brief smile, she said quietly, 'That was thoughtful of you. I'd love to see more of Barcelona before we go.'

'Now,' Luis said suddenly, causing her to start, 'what would you like to see?' Now, she had to look up and found him studying her over the rim of his cup.

'As I know so little about Barcelona,' she responded, 'I'll leave it to you.'

'Then perhaps a general tour of the city,' he suggested pleasantly. 'You will have many more opportunities to come again during your stay.'

'I hope so,' she said, managing a smile, 'but as I must go back at the end of the month, I doubt if I shall see as much as I would like.'

'So, once the business side of your visit is completed you intend returning to England?' he asked, frowning.

'Business side? I'd hardly call visiting my grandfather a business venture,' she replied quietly. 'I hope to come again—perhaps next year.'

He made a harsh sound and shrugged. 'Next

34

year could be too late—he may not be with us then.'

'He's only in his seventies,' she protested. 'Many people live far longer.

'Then you are more optimistic than his nurse,' he said. 'But, of course, you in your youthful wisdom will know best.'

'I am a qualified nurse,' she reminded him with a defiant lift of her chin.

'You may have a medical qualification, but if you think that compensates for years of experience, then you are extremely naïve,' he said with a disparaging lift of his brow.

'That is merely your opinion!' she shot back, her eyes sparkling with indignation. 'And may I remind you, I am not a child!'

'I can see that,' he conceded, his voice mocking as his dark gaze slid over her appraisingly.

She shifted uncomfortably in her chair, extremely conscious of his sensuous regard. Yet, curiously, his blatant admiration sent a ripple of excitement through her body.

'Would you like more coffee?' she enquired in a rather breathless voice as she reached forward to take the jug.

Luis appeared about to continue his mockery then, with a flicker of a smile, simply handed her his cup. Her hand shook a little as she took it; never before had she known a man to have such influence over her emotions, stretching her nerves to breaking point each moment she was in his presence.

She pondered again over his reference to the business side of her visit—surely, he didn't consider her an opportunist. Did he think she was visiting her ageing relative to stake some claim on his estate? Initially, according to the solicitor, her grandfather had wanted to meet Serena's mother, the daughter he had never met. On hearing of her death, he had asked instead to meet his granddaughter, Serena. Through the solicitor, he had forwarded her air fare, offering the opportunity of a holiday in the sun for as long as she cared to stay if she would visit him. Intrigued by this mysterious relative, she'd accepted.

She stared into space, not seeing anything in particular. Why had Clive made the arrangement to meet her here in Barcelona and then disappointed her? On reflection, he had been the one most keen on the idea, yet he had let her down, left her disillusioned.

'What are you thinking?' Luis asked suddenly, causing her to spill a little of her coffee into the saucer. 'You seem far away.'

She gave a nervous little laugh. 'Nothing important,' she said convincingly. And, with fingers that still trembled slightly, she dabbed her mouth with her napkin and announced, 'I'm ready when you are.'

'Have you much packing to do?' he asked rising from his chair.

'Not much—it won't take long. And I

mustn't forget to pay my bill before I leave.'

'Don't worry. I attended to that when I ordered breakfast.'

She glanced up in surprise. 'If you tell me how much I owe you—' she began, but he brushed the matter aside with an impatient gesture of his hand.

'Not now,' he said. 'Let's make the most of the beautiful weather. It's a perfect day for our tour of the city.'

Returning the few things she had unpacked to her case, Serena felt an easing of the tension within her. At least there would be plenty to talk about as they toured the city, and Luis was unlikely to ask her any more personal questions. And, once they reached her grandfather's home, Luis's duties as chauffeur would be over. Or would they? She had a feeling she would see more of senor Luis Bachs than she had anticipated . . .

CHAPTER THREE

Driving along with Luis in his expensive car, Serena took in the view. They were travelling along a palm-lined road towards a port, where huge ships lay at anchor in the sun-dappled water.

'Barcelona's port is the largest in Spain,' Luis told her proudly. 'A stopping place for the main Spanish and foreign shipping lines.' And as they drove along, he continued to direct her attention to other interesting features; the tall Columbus colon, the caravel, Santa Maria, a reproduction of Columbus' flag ship, and the over-head cable cars which connected the port with the mountain of Montjuich.

Serena uttered a contented sigh as she looked around her, the warm breeze coming in from the open car window ruffling her hair. And when they reached the foot of the mountain, Luis spoke of the illuminated fountains that played there in the evenings after dark.

'This, you must see,' he said, his eyes bright with enthusiasm. 'It is a spectacle of colour when the fountains dance to the music—and the tallest jets reach almost fifty metres. They are known as the dancing fountains—a spectacle, indeed,' he ended, casting her a sideways glance as he manoeuvred the car through the traffic.

'Sounds fascinating,' she answered, genuinely interested. 'I'd like to see them one evening.'

'Then I shall ensure I am free to drive you at the earliest opportunity,' he promised. 'Perhaps next Saturday.'

'Maybe the family would like to come,' she said.

'I doubt it,' he said flatly. 'My son has seen them many times.'

'You have a son?' she asked with interest. 'Do tell me about him.'

'You didn't know?' He sounded surprised.

'No, I know nothing about you.'

'My son, Genaro, is ten years old and a very normal little boy, though perhaps a trifle mischievous,' he admitted with an indulgent smile.

'And the rest of the family?' she began.

'You will meet Genaro this afternoon,' he said, cutting her off. He pressed his foot hard on the accelerator, driving the car up the steep hill at greater speed.

Once on the mountain, he brought the car to a halt. 'Montjuich,' he told her. 'The mountain of the Jews.' And they left the car to stroll towards the great cannon, a relic of bygone days, pointing out to sea. Here, she followed his gesturing hand as he pointed ahead to where she had a splendid view of the port and the open sea beyond. Continuing their stroll, he took her hand to guide her up the grassy slope, and even when he paused to draw her attention to the view over the sprawling city he retained his warm grip. As they walked on, Serena realised suddenly that she was totally relaxed in Luis's company, for once.

'What will you say to Mr Mortimer when next you meet?' he asked suddenly, coming to a halt on the path. 'Do you forgive easily?'

'Really,' she replied, flushed with indignation, 'it's no concern of yours. I'm quite sure there is a perfectly simple explanation.'

'Such devotion!' he exclaimed softly, his eyes mocking her. 'I hope he appreciates it.'

Serena forced a smile. 'Of course he does. We have been friends for quite a while, you know,' she responded with forced lightness, thinking it wise to remind this dark Latin her affections lay with Clive. Perhaps then, he would keep his distance.

'Yet, last night, when I asked if you loved him, you would not answer,' he reminded her with a quizzical smile.

'Last night was different,' she countered. 'I'd had an extremely trying day.'

'Ah, of course—the matter of the handbag,' he agreed drily as they returned to his car.

'You must agree it was a bad start to my visit,' she protested mildly as she slid into the passenger seat. 'But for you, I would have lost most of my belongings.'

'So, last night's kiss was merely gratitude,' he remarked with deliberate mockery as he took the driver's seat and, turning his darkly assessing gaze in her direction, added, 'Yet, I could have sworn you enjoyed it.'

Quickly averting her eyes to look through the side window, Serena remained silent as he started the engine. Until now it had been a pleasant morning, if only the conversation hadn't become quite so personal. She found Luis's knack of probing her innermost thoughts quite disturbing. Clive had never had this effect upon her, she reflected.

They were almost down into the city again when Luis suggested they continue their drive before having lunch in his restaurant. She noticed he drove expertly, giving information on every place of special interest as they travelled along, the change of topic making conversation easy for her again. And it was with a tinge of regret that she agreed to bring their drive to an end when he reminded her it was time for lunch.

During the meal, Luis explained the menu, laughing as she pulled a wry, face when he suggested snails in garlic, and she found herself completely at ease in the comfortable atmosphere of the dining-room. She laughed with him, the wine relaxing her earlier tension. Or was it the wine? Perhaps Luis's present mood had something to do with it.

But when the meal was over, and it was time

41

for them to leave for her grandfather's house, Serena's cheerful mood left her to be replaced by one of apprehension. She was always nervous of meeting new people, never mind mysterious relatives.

'I will be close by,' he assured her, rising from the table. 'I will be close by if you need me,' he added smilingly as he looked down on her anxious face.

'But don't you live here, in Barcelona?' she asked. 'I thought you said this was your restaurant?'

He laughed. 'Yes, but I live with the family—making wine is my main business. Now, if you will excuse me, I must collect my briefcase before we go.'

During the short time he was gone, Serena remembered she still owed him money for the hotel but decided to wait until they reached his car. However, when she broached the matter, he brushed it aside and started the engine. 'It was my pleasure,' he said, covering her hand as she opened her bag.

'But I must pay my debts,' she protested, taking out her purse.

He glanced sideways, a devilish glint in his eye as he said, 'Then, perhaps a kiss—that would be adequate payment.'

'Must you start all that again?' she returned impatiently, avoiding his gaze.

'Come, come, where is your English sense of humour?' he derided her softly. 'It is supposed to be one of your assets.'

'When you make such remarks, I don't feel at all like laughing,' she countered drily. 'You had your kiss last night, though, as you said earlier, it was merely gratitude.'

'I consider your attitude quite insulting!' he yelled angrily, his accent becoming more pronounced.

'Now who's lost his sense of humour?' she retorted coldly. 'You surprise me, Luis!'

He shot her a threatening glance and said with soft menace, 'You will regret provoking me, Serena—now, let's get moving!'

It took Serena a while to simmer down after that, and she remained rigidly upright in her seat. Luis, silent beside her, accelerated fiercely as they travelled out of the busy city and into the country on roads that were sometimes narrow and rough. She felt confused by his change of mood, hardly noticing the rows of fruit-laden vines lining the roadside or the abundance of bright flowers cascading over the balconies of the white-walled houses they passed.

Suddenly, Luis brought the car to a halt at the roadside and pulled on the brake, his movement drawing her eyes towards him. Turning, he stretched an arm along the back of her seat, his strong features immobile as he studied her face.

'I think it better if we come to some kind of agreement before we reach the house. I would prefer us to appear reasonably friendly on arrival—at least in the presence of other members of the household.'

Serena resisted a sharp retort and merely shrugged. 'That suits me fine,' she responded with forced lightness. 'I certainly don't want to make an enemy of anyone.'

'I am pleased you agree,' he said smoothly as he put the car into gear and drove quickly away, the spinning tyres raising a cloud of dust on the road behind.

Serena relaxed in her seat. Those few words with Luis, however strained, had eased the tension a little though she sensed his acceptance of her presence here was not as easy for him as he would have it appear.

For the next few kilometres she attempted to take more interest in the scenery around her, where, as far as she could see, there were rows of vines on sun-scorched earth.

Then, as they came over the brow of a hill, huge mountains came in to view.

'Montserrat,' Luis told her, nodding ahead. 'There is a monastery high up there, built in the shelter of the rocks. It is well worth a visit, and from the monastery there is a splendid view of the land below.'

'Sounds interesting,' she said and had to admit, 'I never expected scenery quite so beautiful as this.'

He made no comment and merely smiled, his eyes crinkling attractively at the corners, and a little further along the road he again directed her attention through the windscreen.

'See the house beyond the trees?' he asked. 'That is were we are heading.'

As they drew near, Serena saw it was a very large building, partly hidden by a high wall and surrounded by vineyards. And when they turned off the road to pass beneath an archway in the wall, she had a clear view of the impressive architecture.

By stone steps leading up to a heavily-carved, wooden door, Luis brought the car to a standstill, and he had barely alighted when there came a whoop of joy and a young dark-haired boy ran out from the side of the house.

'Papa, Papa!' the child shrieked delightedly, flinging himself into Luis's arms then, spotting Serena, he released his father and fixed her with a solemn stare.

'This is my son, Genaro,' Luis said with a proud smile as he drew the boy round the car to where she was standing. 'He does speak a little English.'

Serena smiled and offered her hand. The boy gave a small, formal bow and a polite greeting in his own tongue.

'As I have already told you, Genaro, Miss Ferguson is a distant relative of your grandfather. She is to stay with us for a while,' Luis explained to his son and, turning to Serena, he told her, 'Genaro will help you familiarise yourself with your new surroundings.'

'Thank you. I'll be grateful for your help, Genaro,' she said, smiling down at the boy. But his only response was a petulant shrug as he shot her a hostile glance, his dark brown eyes exactly like those of his father.

'You must excuse Genaro. He is a little shy,' Luis explained with an indulgent smile as he ruffled the boy's hair and suggested he go and inform the cook of their arrival.

'He looks very like you,' Serena remarked as Luis lifted her case from the boot of his car.

'Yes, yet you appear to lack the really dark features of your ancestors,' he commented as he ushered her up the steps.

Was he doubting she was a true relative of her grandfather, Senor Miguel Artigas, she wondered as she followed him into the panelled hall. He had not asked for proof of her identity, unless he had confirmed that for himself from the contents of her bag.

Luis paused as someone came through a door at the rear of the hall. By their conversation, she realised this must be the cook, Rosa, and she murmured a greeting in Spanish. Warming to the old cook's smile, Serena relaxed a little as Luis explained how Rosa had served the family for years and had become indispensable to the household.

'This is a beautiful house,' Serena commented when the cook withdrew, and she let her gaze wander to the ceiling where a huge

46

chandelier hung from its centre, the crystal pendants sparkling in the broad shaft of sunlight streaming in through the open front door.

'It is almost two hundred years old,' Luis informed her with a casual shrug. 'I am surprised someone so young should appreciate the beauty of an old building.'

'Of course I do,' she returned. 'In fact, the panelling is a work of art. Such wonderful craftsmanship. It must be worth a fortune.'

'Ah! I see you don't underestimate the value,' he said with a wry smile. 'I expect you will wish to see all the valuable works of art in the house, yes?'

Serena gave a little frown. 'In case you are worried, I don't intend to burgle the place,' she said with a short laugh.

'Of course,' he responded with a tight smile. 'I had not considered burglary as being your object.'

Serena shot him a curious look. What a strange thing for him to say—perhaps something had got lost in his use of English. Mentally shrugging away her feeling of unease, she asked, 'How soon may I see my grandfather? I'll admit I'm nervous but I'm longing to meet him.'

'At the moment, he is sleeping,' Luis informed her, glancing up the wide staircase, 'but he should be awake by the time you have unpacked. Tomas will take up your luggage,

and after you have rested we can meet in the
sala—about five-thirty?'

Reluctantly, Serena agreed. Eager as she
was, she didn't want to disturb the old man's
rest, and it would be nice to change before
they met, as she wanted to look her best for
this first meeting.

Serena's room was at the front of the house.
It was well furnished and spacious with a tiled
bathroom en suite; an immaculate room that
appeared rarely used. By the stillness of the
house she assumed the other members of the
family were resting; she very quietly unpacked
her case, sorting her clothes in the huge,
mahogany wardrobe. She felt much too
impatient to consider a rest and took more
time than usual choosing a dress to wear.
Finally, slipping into one of a silky blue
material that fell into soft folds below her trim
waist, she brushed her hair to gleaming
smoothness and took out a pink lipstick,
noticing her hand shook a little as she applied
it. Ridiculous to be so nervous, really. Then,
taking a deep breath, she prepared to meet
Luis downstairs.

She found him staring out onto the patio
where Genaro was curled up in a cane chair
reading a book. And, when Luis turned at her
approach, she saw in his eyes a far-away look,
a certain sadness in his expression as he
murmured a welcome. He had changed into
more casual clothes; a black shirt with the

sheen of silk, and dark slim-fitting slacks that accentuated his long muscular legs as he advanced towards her with almost cat-like grace.

'You look most charming, Serena,' he said, his thoughtful expression melting away as he drew her further into the room and motioned to her to take one of the large, comfortable chairs. 'What will you have to drink?'

'Maybe a local wine, please,' she stammered, avoiding his look as she took her seat.

'Of course, from our own vineyard,' he agreed, filling a glass with pale, golden liquid that sparkled in the light.

Taking the drink and a few of the tiny biscuits he invited her to try, she glanced round the room, searching her mind for something suitable to say. She thought it strange his wife had not yet put in an appearance, though hadn't the courage to mention it; Luis may get the impression she was nervous of being alone with him. Come to think of it, she was; even his son had disappeared after spotting her in the room.

'It's very quiet here,' she managed finally, taking another biscuit from the dish.

'Nervous, Serena?' he enquired, his lips twitching with amusement as he twirled his glass in his long, tanned fingers.

'Of course not,' she denied. 'I was just wondering where everyone was.'

49

'When the harvest begins there will be much more activity around the house,' he told her and went on to add that he would soon be out in the vineyards each day when people from local villages would be employed to pick the grapes.

Much to her relief, he continued to speak of daily matters, including the nurse who was in constant attendance to her grandfather—a local woman who had acted as midwife in the past.

'Do you think my grandfather will be awake now?' she asked when she saw Luis glance at his watch.

'Nurse will let you know when he is ready to receive you,' he stated with an air of authority. 'We don't interfere with her routine if we can avoid it.'

'Of course,' Serena murmured and into her mind came a picture of a woman in a starched apron, brisk and efficient, like some of the older ward sisters she had encountered during her training. But this picture was not nearly as formidable as the woman who entered the lounge moments later. To Serena, it was almost as if they had gone back in time by half a century when she saw the nurse, a rigid figure dressed in black with iron-grey hair pulled tightly into a coil at the back of her head.

'Senor Miguel will see the senorita now,' she announced in Spanish. 'But I can only allow a few minutes. He is very weak.'

Luis translated, then replied to the nurse, before turning to Serena to say, 'If you follow nurse, she will take you to his room.'

Serena followed the stiff-backed woman up the wide staircase, and as they passed along the corridor above, asked timidly, 'How is Senor Miguel?'

'You will see,' the nurse replied coldly, without turning. 'But you must not tire my patient, he is difficult as it is.'

Serena stayed silent. Perhaps later, she would mention her own career—they had something in common—but this hardly seemed the moment to speak of it. Half-way along the corridor the nurse paused and pushed open a door, signalling for her to enter. With rising apprehension, Serena went into the large room, which at first seemed uninhabited. But as she moved closer to the great bed, she saw the frail figure of an old man lying beneath the sheets, his head hardly visible on the low, thin pillow. Swallowing hard, she moved softly to the head of the bed, voicing a gentle greeting as she drew near. The figure didn't stir but a pair of bright dark eyes fixed upon her and she heard her name spoken in a weak and wavering voice.

'Yes, Grandfather, it's Serena,' she responded gently, laying her hand on his and stroking the almost transparent skin which covered the prominent bones. 'How are you

51

feeling?' she asked, giving his hand a gentle squeeze. But the old man merely shook his head and she saw a large tear escape and run along his cheek.

Again the lump rose in Serena's throat, but she managed to retain her smiling expression. 'I'm so pleased to meet you, Grandfather,' she continued, striving to keep the emotion from her voice. 'I'm sad that my mother couldn't have made this journey, too, though I am so delighted you wished to see me.'

To Serena's dismay, tears flowed freely from his eyes and when he gave a weak cough, she was shocked to note the poor condition of his chest. Deciding he ought not to be lying so low in the bed, she reached for a cushion in a nearby chair and, easing him up a little, slid it under his pillow. Then, taking a clean tissue from her bag, she dabbed the tears from his eyes.

'There,' she said softly, 'does that feel better? I must admit, I feel a little choked up, too.' She gave him a tremulous smile.

'Serena,' the old man croaked, 'stay with me.' And he clung weakly to her hand.

'Of course I will,' she agreed to his tearful appeal. 'While I'm here, I'll spend all my time with you. We have lots to talk about, I'm sure.'

'You will stay?' he asked again, his breathing a little easier now. 'I have no-one but you and Luis, and the boy.'

'I promise. I'll stay until you are much

better,' she said, smiling as she smoothed his thick, greying hair. 'We have to get to know each other.'

He shook his head, weakly. 'It is too late,' he whispered. 'I should have sent for you a long time ago.'

'Nonsense.' Serena rebuked him gently. 'You'll be fine, you'll see—' Hearing the door open she broke off and, turning towards it, saw the unsmiling figure of his nurse.

'You have overstayed your time, senorita,' she said, icily authoritative. 'Senor Miguel becomes exhausted by too much chatter—I must insist you leave, immediately.'

Reluctantly, Serena rose and bent to place a kiss on her grandfather's cheek. 'I'll see you later,' she promised softly and, with a wave of her hand, she crossed the room to where the nurse was waiting, pointedly holding open the door.

'Tomorrow, senorita,' the nurse said stiffly, 'will be soon enough.'

Serena sighed. It had become increasingly clear to her that she and the nurse were not going to get along very well. Apart from the nurse's attitude, Serena wasn't happy about the way he was being cared for, if his position in the bed was an indication of the nurse's skills. Even the lowest student nurse knows that a patient with congested lungs should be propped up with lots of pillows.

Just as Serena descended the stairs, the

cook came into the hall, a ready smile on her round, olive-skinned face. 'Have you seen the senor?' Rosa asked. 'I know he would be happy to see you, yes?'

'Yes, I have just left him, but I'm afraid his nurse was not so pleased,' Serena told her with a rueful sigh.

'Pah!' Rosa exclaimed with a dismissive shrug, then, with a sad little shake of her head, added, 'The poor man is very weak, and he eats so little, no matter what I prepare to tempt him.'

'I'm sure you do all you can,' Serena agreed, 'but I think he is too ill to have any appetite. Perhaps I can help persuade him to take a little more.'

'Senor Luis spends much of his time encouraging him to eat,' Rosa imparted with a despairing lift of her plump shoulders, 'also Genaro when he is at home.'

'And his wife, Senora Bachs,' Serena ventured, 'does she help to care for her father?'

For a moment Rosa only stared, her shocked expression startling Serena, particularly when the cook went on to lift a work-worn hand to touch her forehead, then chest, in the sign of the cross. But, before she could press the cook further, Luis strode through the front door and Rosa quickly withdrew to the kitchens.

'Gossiping already!' Luis exclaimed, lightly

54

enough, though Serena detected a harsh note in the bright tone.

'We were merely speaking about my grandfather's appetite,' she explained, following him into the sitting-room. 'In fact, I'm very concerned about him. He doesn't look at all well and I would like to speak to you about him when you have a moment.'

'Of course,' he agreed. 'And if you would like to accompany me to the bodega, we can talk as we go. It will give you the opportunity to see part of the vineyard.'

They set off in the warmth of the early evening sun, across the wide garden and out through a gate at the rear of the house. Here, he led her through an orchard—apple, peach and pear trees—the fruits long picked, a few lying on the ground beneath them. The warm air was filled with the scent of flowers and fruit and Luis smiled when she paused to breathe in the delightful fragrance.

'What was it you wished to ask about your grandfather?' he queried, coming to lean against the stone wall bordering a well. 'Has seeing him caused you to feel upset?' he remarked, frowning.

'Yes, it has,' she admitted, her brow furrowed by concern as she looked up at Luis. 'It wasn't just seeing him that upset me. I'm a little worried about the way he's being looked after. What does the doctor have to say?'

'The nurse tells me there is little that can be

done to help him now,' Luis told her with a saddening expression. 'She would only call the doctor in an emergency.'

'But this is an emergency!' Serena cried in dismay. 'He ought to have medication for his chest, and he should not be kept lying flat on his back—he should be propped up in bed, if not out in a chair.'

'The nurse came to us with sound recommendation,' Luis pointed out, 'and I am sure she has a great deal of experience with such cases. Naturally, I am concerned for his welfare, but don't you think you are exaggerating the situation rather? After all, he's not a young man.'

'Certainly not!' she responded firmly, meeting his confused gaze. 'This nurse may have years of experience but, in case you hadn't realised, I am qualified. I spent three years in training and some of it was with cases similar to his. I'd feel much happier if you would call his doctor. He would confirm I'm telling you the truth.'

'Very well, if you really consider it will help him,' he conceded with a faintly puzzled frown. 'I must admit to having little knowledge of illnesses such as his. His regular practitioner retired some time ago but I am sure his successor will have his notes.'

'Thank you. Maybe I could speak with the doctor when he calls. He may wish me to help out, to give the nurse a break,' Serena said.

'She must get extremely tired.'

'So you want to keep in practice, eh?' He smiled, but added perceptively, 'Or is it that you don't trust the nurse?'

Before she could reply, a shout came from the direction of the house. 'Papa! Papa! Telephone!'

Excusing himself, Luis strode off towards the house, leaving Serena with a bemused smile lingering on her lips. She was pleased he had agreed to call a doctor and, apart from the occasional sarcastic comment, he appeared to be making an effort to be pleasant, though she guessed he wasn't finding it easy. And yet, when she thought of the rather calculating way he'd made a pass at her, she wondered.

Leaning against the stone well, she closed her eyes as the vivid memory of his kiss returned. The firm caress of his long fingers and soft lips were still clear in her mind . . .

Suddenly, she came out of her reverie as a small figure drew near and a pair of haunting dark eyes caught hers, compelling her attention. It was Genaro who stood a short distance away, his face twitching with emotion as he uttered a harsh tirade in his own tongue.

'He's my grandfather!' he shrieked, his young face contorted with pain. 'We don't want you here. Go away!' Then he ran off, through the orchard, leaving Serena to stare after him in stunned silence.

Too shocked to call after him, Serena felt an

icy tremor run through her as the full impact of his words penetrated her brain. Was it merely childish jealousy which had caused such an outburst, or could he have overheard a remark of his father's?

With Genaro's words still ringing in her ears, she turned hastily towards the house. She had to avoid Luis until she'd had time to recover. He doted on the boy, so it was better he didn't know. But, too late, he came through the orchard gate just as she approached it, his expression grim as he confronted her.

'Genaro is terribly upset,' he said icily. 'What did you say to him?'

'What did I say?' she exclaimed in astonishment, her voice shaking with emotion. 'I think you should ask yourself the reason why your son is upset, senor!' And, with a determined lift of her chin, she added, 'Perhaps it would be better if I took a room in the village and visited my grandfather when you are not at home. I have no wish to intrude upon this household, as you so obviously don't want me here!'

CHAPTER FOUR

With a toss of her head, Serena made a move towards the house, her eyes averted so that Luis should not see the angry tears about to spill down her cheeks. But Luis was too quick for her and, catching her wrist in his powerful fingers, he brought her back beside him.

'I thought we'd agreed not to argue,' he reminded her through clenched teeth.

'That was in the presence of your family,' she shot back, jerking her arm free. 'And, considering you have just accused me of upsetting your son, when it was the other way round, what do you expect?'

'I did not expect to have an hysterical young woman on my hands,' he returned and, in a remarkably controlled voice, added, 'and it is my responsibility to deal with any problems that occur.'

'But I am not your responsibility, senor,' she reminded him coldly. 'I am not your wife.'

'No. My wife died some years ago,' he said hollowly, and he walked on, along the dusty path through the orchard.

Struck by remorse, Serena hurried after him. 'I'm terribly sorry, I had no idea . . .' she began as she reached his side. 'No-one told me.'

'I am surprised!' he exclaimed with sarcasm

as he shot her a sideways glance. 'I assumed you to be quite familiar with the history of this family.'

'I wouldn't have been so tactless if I'd known,' she assured him. 'I'm not that insensitive.'

Luis came to a sudden halt and, looking down on her, remarked, 'I find it difficult to decide if you are sincere or merely a clever actress.'

Supressing her indignation, Serena looked him straight in the eye. 'I may have been tactless,' she admitted, 'but please don't doubt my sincerity, Luis.'

'Then we will say no more abut it,' he said shortly, before walking on in silence until they left the trees, coming to a huge area of dry ground densely covered by fruit-laden vines.

Now, as Luis scanned the vines, his expression told her little of his thoughts. But he didn't appear to have any feelings of animosity towards her when he gestured over the vast area before them and spoke of the promise of a good crop.

'It must be very satisfying,' she remarked, noting the lines of tension had eased from his face.

'I don't find it quite so interesting now we are mechanised,' he told her. 'Less exhausting, of course, but I liked the old days. It was almost an art, one could say,' he ended on a faraway note.

'Has my grandfather always been involved in wine-making?' she asked as they circled the orchard in the direction of the bodega.

'Almost always, except during the civil war. Being landowners, his family were not too happy about his activities during those years but, once it was over, they welcomed him home. He was a bit of a rebel in those days, I understand.'

Serena smiled. It was difficult to imagine the ailing old man she had only just met to ever have been a rebel, though she noticed Luis spoke of him with affection in his tone. 'It must please him to have you to keep the business going now he is unable to work,' she commented and, indicating the bodega not too far ahead, asked, 'Why do you bother to keep the restaurant when you have all this? I would have thought there is already more than enough work here.'

He shot her a dark, questioning glance. 'Do you mean work, Serena, or profit?'

'Well, both, I suppose,' she replied, wavering a little at his tone. 'It must be a great responsibility.'

'The restaurant was part of my inheritance. I had considered selling, but now that Genaro's future security is questionable . . .' Luis hesitated, then shrugged. With a faint note of sarcasm, he continued, 'But of course, that will not concern you.'

Serena frowned, unable to follow his

meaning but, deciding it wiser not to pursue the matter, remarked with a smile, 'I see, so it's not just business—there is a little sentiment involved.'

'My dear Serena,' he began in a mildly patronising way, 'there is no sentiment in business, I would have thought *you* knew that!'

The emphasis he put on those final words caused her to glance at him in quick surprise, but he didn't elaborate.

The heavy wooden doors of the cellar stood open as they approached, allowing a broad shaft of sunlight to enter the dark interior of the building. Inside, she watched the men at work while Luis had a word with each man in turn. And, although their conversation sounded relaxed, she could tell from their manner they held their employer in high regard.

Leaving the men to continue with their work, they toured the vast building, Luis pointing out the fermentation vats, huge metal cylinders towering above them which would soon be filled with grape juice. He then led her back into the sunlight to an open gantry where, he explained, cart-loads of grapes would be brought in for the first stage of wine-making to begin.

Luis soon had her so interested in the topic of wine production that the incident with Genaro was temporarily forgotten. Perhaps it was wiser to let the matter drop, she thought, as they returned to the house and she saw the child peeping down from an upstairs window. If her grandfather and Luis were the only family he had, he was sure to be possessive about them.

'We dine quite late,' Luis said as they went indoors. 'But if you are hungry, I'll ask Rosa to prepare something.'

'No, please,' Serena answered. 'We had such a large lunch. I would quite like to see my grandfather before dinner, though.'

'Of course,' Luis agreed. 'He eats a little earlier now so that Genaro or myself can join him and try to encourage him to eat a little more.'

'Perhaps I can help,' Serena put in eagerly. 'It will give you a break during the harvest, when you'll be busy enough.'

'In a few minutes I shall be joining him for an aperitif,' Luis told her, glancing at his watch. 'Though even a sherry has lost its appeal for him, these days.'

'Before you go,' Serena began, her hand on his sleeve, 'you won't forget to ring the doctor, will you?'

Luis gave her a brief smile, lowering his gaze to where her hand rested on his arm. 'I won't forget,' he promised. 'I always keep my word.'

'I'm sure you do,' she murmured, quickly withdrawing her hand as she turned towards the wide staircase with Luis following close

63

behind.

As they entered her grandfather's room, the nurse glanced up and rose, her expression one of obvious displeasure. 'Senor Luis, all this coming and going is too much for my patient,' she bristled, casting Serena an unwelcome glance. 'He is not used to having strangers visit so often in one day.'

'The senorita is his granddaughter,' Luis reminded the woman with a touch of impatience. 'And she is also a qualified nurse, so please don't worry about the senor.'

The woman grunted disparagingly and gave Serena a scathing look. 'A nurse!' she exclaimed in disbelief. 'And just how much experience will she have at her age?'

Luis quickly drew the woman out of Senor Miguel's hearing. 'I must ask you to keep a polite tongue in your head, senora!' Serena heard him hiss and, holding open the door, he directed, 'Please leave us, now.'

During this exchange, Serena was watching her grandfather as he struggled out of a doze. She noted the ragged lifting of his bony chest as he breathed and saw twinges of pain cross his face as he tried to ease his position in the bed. He hadn't slept comfortably; she could tell. The nurse should have observed his discomfort as she watched over him from her chair, only a short distance from the bed.

'Grandfather, it's Serena,' she whispered when he was finally awake. 'I have come to sit

64

with you for a while.'

The old man stared at her, his eyes bright beneath dark, bushy brows, then smiled as Luis brought a tray of drinks to place on the bedside table. 'Only water for me, Luis,' he croaked, taking rasping breaths with each word he spoke.

'Before you have a drink, let me put you in a more comfortable position,' Serena suggested and, placing a firm hand beneath the old man's shoulders, she lifted him forward and filled the space behind him with pillows.

Senor Miguel reached out to take her hand as she gently released him, his trembling fingers cool against her skin. 'That is better,' he gasped. 'Now I can see you.' And, to Serena's surprise, he went on to exclaim, 'Madre de Dios! You are beautiful! Don't you agree, Luis?'

Serena met Luis's mocking gaze as she took the sherry he had poured for her. 'Yes, she is beautiful,' he agreed softly and, raising his glass, said, 'To you, Serena.'

'To us all,' Serena responded, her cheeks growing pink. And, attempting to bring a lighter note to the moment, ended, 'And to the grape harvest.'

'How thoughtful,' Luis murmured and, with that same mocking stare, added cryptically—'A toast to your future, one could say.'

Ignoring what she considered to be a rather curious remark, she took a sip of her sherry.

'Like it?' the old man asked and, when she nodded, he continued breathlessly, 'Maria-Sofia brings it from her bodega in Jerez. You will meet her next week.'

'Next week!' Luis exclaimed. 'I shall be much too busy to entertain her.'

'Serena will be here,' the older man pointed out. 'I notice she has a little Spanish.'

'And she'll need it!' Luis exclaimed under his breath as he placed his empty glass on the tray.

Serena shot him a questioning glance but he didn't enlighten her further. 'I'll manage,' she returned softly but wondered if this Marie-Sofia her grandfather spoke of would turn out to be one of those matriarchal figures that ruled many a Spanish household.

Luis merely shrugged and, rising to his feet, said, 'You must excuse me. I have a few telephone calls to make—including the one you mentioned, Serena.'

It took Senor Miguel a while to get his breath after the short conversation and Serena did not wish to over-tire him on her first day. There were so many things she wanted to ask—so much she didn't know—but she had to suppress her curiosity until he was in better health.

Shortly, Rosa arrived with a bowl of soup and stared at the patient in surprise as she placed it on the bed-tray. 'I have not seen you sitting up so well in ages, senor!' she exclaimed happily. 'How you have taken food almost lying down, I will never know.' And, as she was leaving the room, Rosa asked, 'Shall I call nurse?'

'No, thank you,' Serena declined quickly, horrified by the cook's earlier comment, 'I shall stay here until dinner.'

Putting her grandfather's untouched sherry aside, Serena uncovered the tray, pleased to see how daintily it was set. She took the lid off the soup bowl and allowed it to stand a while until it was cool enough to drink. But, after the first spoonful her grandfather shook his head, declaring he had no appetite, and lay back exhausted.

'Don't worry,' she soothed. 'Have a rest now.' Then she dabbed his lips with the linen napkin and removed the tray.

When Luis returned, Senor Miguel was sleeping. 'Doctor Ferrer will be here within the hour, so you will have the opportunity to speak to him—that is, if you are staying?'

Serena glanced up, a trifle ashamed of her earlier outburst. 'When I said I was leaving, I was angry and upset,' she admitted. 'I would like to stay, at least until Grandfather's a little better. Is that OK?'

'Of course—it was Senor Miguel's wish that you stay here, Serena.'

'But not yours, is that right?'

'My only wish is that every consideration should be given towards Senor Miguel's recovery and happiness,' Luis stated without a trace of emotion.

When the nurse came back into the room, Serena went downstairs to await the doctor's arrival. From the sitting-room she heard a car draw up outside, then heard Luis and the doctor go up to her grandfather's room. After about twenty minutes Luis came in to the room with a young, good-looking man who he introduced as Doctor Ferrer. She was relieved to hear the doctor spoke English reasonably well, so she was able to discuss her grandfather without Luis having to act as interpreter. Even so, Luis stayed with them, taking a great interest in what the doctor had to say.

'So can you help him, doctor?' Luis asked when Doctor Ferrer had delivered his diagnosis. 'Senor Miguel has not been well for weeks.'

'I am sure we can, though had I been called earlier, it would have been a much more simple matter to treat him,' Doctor Ferrer told Luis. 'However, when you gave me his symptoms over the telephone, I came prepared. A course of these tablets should soon bring about some improvement,' he ended, taking a small bottle from his case.

Serena took the bottle and queried its contents, and when the doctor explained the drug in more detail she nodded, saying, 'I've used these before—they're very good.'

Luis rose and smacked his fist into the palm

of his other hand. 'I should have called you earlier!' he exclaimed angrily. 'But his nurse assured me nothing could be done for a man of his years.'

'I'm afraid her ideas are rather outdated,' Ferrer remarked. 'She considers death inevitable for anyone Senor Miguel's age. However, I've given her strict instructions to keep her patient more upright in his bed—and to watch out for pressure sores which can be very uncomfortable.'

'Don't worry, doctor. I'll make sure he is property nursed,' Serena said, resisting a triumphant glance at Luis.

Promising to call again in the morning, the doctor left, leaving Serena a great deal happier with the situation. Doctor Ferrer appeared to be a thorough and competent man who had every hope of his patient making a full recovery.

'I'll hire another nurse,' Luis said firmly after he had seen the doctor out. 'But this time, it will be someone fully trained.'

'Just a minute!' Serena interjected sharply. 'Have you no confidence in me? I also want to see my grandfather well again and, personally, intend to nurse him back to health, whoever you decide to employ.'

CHAPTER FIVE

The following morning, Serena rose early and prepared to join her grandfather. She had arranged with Rose to have all her meals, with the exception of late dinner, in his room, so that she could keep a close watch on his progress. This also meant she didn't have to share the breakfast and lunch table with Luis and suffer any further cutting comments he was likely to make.

This morning, Senor Miguel looked both pleased and relieved to see her from where he lay, almost flat, on one thin pillow. This was something she had anticipated and, regardless of the nurse's disapproval, she again raised him on a pile of professionally-arranged pillows, noting his gasp of relief.

'The doctor said he should not lie flat,' she reminded the nurse in her halting Spanish. 'We should do as he says.'

'Pah!' the woman retorted acidly as she bustled about the room. 'All these modern ideas . . .'

Serena ignored the nurse's mutterings, concentrating on persuading her grandfather to drink a little. And she was pleased when the doctor arrived to repeat his instructions to the other nurse. Satisfied that Serena had personally ensured that the patient had taken the drug prescribed, Doctor Ferrer left, promising to call again later.

At mid-day, when Rosa brought in lunch, she informed Serena that Senor Luis wished to see her downstairs as soon as she had eaten. Serena sighed. She had been so engrossed in her caring duties, she had not allowed him to enter her thoughts and now felt a wave of dismay over having to face him again. She was aware he had looked in on his father-in-law when she was out of the room and had assumed he wished to avoid her. So why did he seek her company now?

Going downstairs, she found Luis in the dining-room, the larger portion of his meal unnoticed. He motioned to her to take a chair as he poured a drink into a small glass.

'Have a drink,' he offered finally, handing her the glass. 'And for goodness sake, Serena, sit down!'

She had been about to decline his offer but he didn't appear to be in the mood for argument and, as she sank down on the chair, he tossed a letter on the table in front of her; a letter bearing an English stamp.

'It arrived about twenty minutes ago,' he told her, his dark eyes assessing her reaction. 'I assume the sender is Mortimer?'

Serena glanced down at the typewritten envelope and knew that, although Luis sounded casual, he was tense and watchful. However, with a devilish urge to let him

71

assume what he wished, she thanked him and pushed the letter to one side.

'Doctor Ferrer was quite pleased with his patient this morning,' she offered lightly. 'And you will be pleased to know the nurse is now carrying out his instructions.'

'Good!' Luis responded shortly, his gaze straying to the unopened letter as he rose and said, 'Obviously, you would prefer to read your letter in private.' And he left the room.

Turning the wine glass thoughtfully in her fingers, Serena studied the long envelope. She knew it wasn't from Clive—he never used her letters of qualification after her name—so it had to be from the hospital, where she had left a forwarding address. Going to the window, she drew back the heavy curtains to allow more light into the room and, taking a knife from the drawer of the beautifully-carved sideboard, she slit open the envelope.

As she expected, the letter had been sent from her London hospital offering her the opportunity to apply for a senior position in the children's unit, and she was relieved to note that the closing date for the application wasn't until the day after she was due to fly back. She needed this time to consider both the health of her grandfather and the responsibilities of her new post. She couldn't possibly leave until she was certain he was well on the way to recovery.

Serena found conversation with Luis over

dinner that evening to be rather a strain and she was relieved when the meal came to an end.

'Well?' Luis said finally as she rose from the table. 'Has Mortimer managed to provide an acceptable excuse?'

'He hasn't tried!' she retorted. 'And I wish you wouldn't keep reminding me ...'

Luis glanced up, his eyes darkly menacing. 'Hasn't tried!' he exploded. 'He wrote you a letter without offering a plausable explanation for his absence, and you accept it? Madre de Dios!'

'It wasn't from Clive!' she cried furiously. 'And you had no right to presume it was. You can read it if you wish.'

Disregarding her offer, he continued to glare at her as he rose to his feet. 'I find it strange he has not contacted you,' he said.

'Perhaps so. So do I,' she agreed shortly. 'Actually, as you're so interested, the letter contains a possible chance of promotion.'

'You will take it?' he asked in a more controlled voice.

She shrugged. 'It's tempting but, as I told you before, it depends on the state of my grandfather's health.'

'Do you mean state, or estate?' he interjected swiftly. 'No promotion of yours could possibly equal his wealth, as well you know.'

'How dare you!' she cried indignantly, hot

colour flushing her cheeks.

'I'd like to believe you, Serena,' he responded with deliberate mockery as he moved towards the door, 'but I suspect your presence here is something Mortimer contrived.'

The door had slammed behind him before Serena had the chance to retaliate and, overcome by angry indignation, she sank down on her chair. How dare Luis Bachs accuse her of being here to profit from her grandfather's estate. She knew her bank account never rose far above a few hundred pounds, but she had her pride.

She remembered that Clive had indeed shown quite an interest in the status of her elderly relative after the solicitor had first approached her about the matter, but Luis wasn't to know that.

Stifling a sob of frustration, she determined to put the matter straight with Luis at the first opportunity, by convincing him she intended to leave once her grandfather was sufficiently improved. She could appreciate that Luis, quite naturally, would expect his son to be the sole beneficiary and it must have come as a shock to him to learn that Genaro was not the only grandchild. She tried to excuse his insulting manner as being that of a protective father who displayed a good measure of Latin temperament. And yet, during that first evening in Barcelona, his approach had been anything but that of a challenging relative.

Her lower lip quivered as she mounted the stairs, recalling the turmoil of the past two days. But, as she smoothed her grandfather's bed and placed a good-night kiss on his cheek, she knew, for his sake, it was all worthwhile.

*   *   *

Doctor Ferrer was pleased with his patient's progress and continued to make daily visits during the next few days. Serena kept a constant watch over her grandfather, administering her professional care and even his own nurse responded with a begrudging but silent efficiency to the doctor's wishes. Luis visited his father-in-law two or three times each day though he carefully avoided including Serena in their conversation, or acknowledging she was in the room.

Genaro usually called on his grandfather when she was out of the room, except for one afternoon when she was sitting quietly in the easy chair and Genaro wasn't aware she was there to witness his show of affection. The child had entered the room and moved softly over to the bed to place a kiss on the cheek of its sleeping occupant, and it had brought a lump to her throat to see her grandfather stir and reach out a hand to touch the boy's dark head. Suddenly, Genaro had become aware she was there, his dark brown eyes wide with surprise, but, to prevent him darting from the room, she spoke to him gently, giving him a simple update about his grandfather's progress. After that, Genaro became a little more friendly towards her which pleased her a great deal.

Each day, Senor Miguel gained in health and, to Serena's delight, took his first few tottering steps since her arrival.

And she continued to make progress with Genaro, who treated her with a kind of awesome respect now his grandfather was back to his more normal self. The only shadow cast over her pleasure was Luis's attitude towards her on the few occasions their paths met. He treated her with a cool indifference, ate at irregular times, and avoided visiting Senor Miguel when she was there. Not that she really cared, she told herself, but she didn't want to make enemies of anyone, particularly as she didn't consider herself at fault.

By the beginning of the second week, Senor Miguel was able to move around his room and, for a few hours each day, he would sit beside the open balcony windows which looked out on to a flower-filled terrace. And now, Serena noticed something different about Luis. His sarcastic indifference to her had been replaced by a quiet and rather anxious approach that she couldn't understand. She wondered if the grape harvest was not going as well as he had expected.

'It is wonderful to see you looking so well,' Serena told her grandfather one morning after she had persuaded him to spend some time out on the terrace.

'Does that mean you will soon be leaving me?' he ventured shrewdly as she arranged his cushions. 'Luis tells me you have had the offer of promotion in England.'

'Yes, that's true,' she admitted, 'but I haven't even sent my application yet.' And, as she made him comfortable, she realised she'd been so absorbed in her caring duties, she had made no effort to reply to the letter.

'Then why not stay here with me?' he suggested hopefully. 'I can provide for you—everything you need . . .'

'Grandfather, I couldn't,' she protested quickly. 'Please don't ask me again. I'll come and visit you, of course, but I couldn't just leave the hospital like that. I love my work.'

'I know Luis will be sorry to see you go,' he commented thoughtfully.

Serena laughed. 'Nonsense, Grandfather! Once you are well again, he won't even notice I'm not here.'

'Poor Luis,' the old man sighed as he took up the newspaper Luis had left earlier. 'Poor Luis . . .'

'Yes, it was sad about his wife . . . er, your daughter,' she put in sympathetically. 'I didn't know until Luis told me.'

'We were devastated,' he agreed quietly.

77

'But Luis gave me the strength to carry on and stayed with me so that I should not be parted from my grandson. After my wife died, and then my daughter, Genaro was all I had. But now you have come into my life, Serena, I am a happy man.'

Serena gripped his hand and fought back her tears, knowing she could never reveal to him the bitterness between Luis and herself. To hear her grandfather speak so highly of him had brought to her a curious kind of warmth.

'I understand it was only recently you revealed you had another daughter,' she ventured, but, seeing his smile fade, added quickly, 'Sorry, Grandfather. I shouldn't have mentioned it if it upsets you.'

The old man sighed deeply as he hung on to her hand. 'You have a right to know about her, my dear,' he assured her gently. 'After all, she was your mother.'

'Yet, I hardly knew anything about her family until a few weeks before she died, and even then it was only to learn that my grandmother never married,' Serena admitted. 'It was the solicitor who told me about you.'

'I met your grandmother towards the end of the Spanish Civil War,' he began, a faraway look coming to his eyes. 'It was during the bombing of Barcelona—I was injured and taken to the hospital, where she was helping to care for the wounded.'

'But how did she come to be there?' Serena asked, becoming more intrigued.

'Her parents had brought her from England. You see, her father was a reporter for one of the daily newspapers and he was always in the thick of battle so the women helped in the hospital,' he explained, uttering a soft groan as the memories returned. 'You can never imagine what it was like in those days, Serena—fighting in the streets, Italian planes overhead, a city divided, and people left to die unless those brave women took them in.'

Serena shuddered. 'How dreadful for you,' she murmured, 'so much fighting and bloodshed . . .'

He shook his head, thoughtfully. 'Yes, they were dreadful times, but your grandmother cared for me well and over the weeks we picked up a little of each other's language, and eventually we fell in love.'

Serena smiled but, not wishing to break his train of thought, remained silent when he continued—'Eventually, I was taken to a house outside the city to recuperate, and Elizabeth, your grandmother, visited me there, bringing food each day. We were so happy together but, during those stressful weeks, our emotions were very vulnerable and . . .' He shook his head and uttered a long wistful sigh, adding, 'I brought shame upon her.'

'But you loved her,' Serena broke in, quite moved by his recollections of so long ago.

'War is a terrible thing, Serena. We planned to marry after it was over, but it parted us. I was sent back to my unit and she and her parents had to flee the city along with thousands of others on that long trek to reach the safety of the French border.' He let out a wavering breath, his head sinking back on the cushions.

'I think you have talked long enough, Grandfather,' she advised, but the old man insisted on adding a little more.

'I didn't know Elizabeth was with child,' he said brokenly, 'until after the war, when I finally managed to contact her family. It was then I learned she had died soon after giving birth to my daughter—the journey had been too much for her —and I was devastated.'

'How very sad,' Serena murmured with feeling. 'And after that, to lose your second daughter . . . You must have been heartbroken.'

Senor Miguel had closed his eyes whilst she was speaking and, with her back to the room, she wasn't aware of Luis standing just inside the doorway. His voice startled her when he said softly, 'I think you should drop the subject now—don't you?'

Quietly, Serena got to her feet and went to confront him in the doorway. 'I'm only asking about my grandmother,' she retorted in a low voice. 'I consider it within my rights.'

'Don't you think it will upset him?' Luis

asked as he retreated into the room.

'Perhaps he needs to talk about the past, occasionally,' she pointed out. 'A little reminiscing rarely does any harm.'

'Perhaps not,' he agreed, 'and I must congratulate you on the quality of care you have given Senor Miguel. You are an excellent nurse, Serena.'

With his hand on the door-knob, he turned and said, 'I expect Father is tired. I'll come back later. By the way, have you made a decision about that post in England?'

'Not yet,' she managed, rather taken aback. 'Why do you ask?'

Luis merely shrugged and said, 'It is entirely your decision, but think carefully.'

'Think carefully,' she echoed blankly, as the door closed behind him, and she realised there was little time left in which to complete her application. But, did she really want to leave? Initially, her visit had been for the sake of her grandfather rather than her own, but now she felt a strong emotional tie with him.

Reluctantly, she set about filling in the application form, knowing it was impossible for her to stay. Her financial resources would not allow it. She had a living to earn and, however much she cared for her grandfather, she could not allow herself to depend on him for support.

With her letter of application safely sealed in an envelope, she went back upstairs to check all was well. A lump rose in her throat as she looked down on her grandfather's sleeping form and, even though the afternoon felt warm, she gently drew a blanket round his legs in case he should feel cool in the shade. Yes, it was going to be hard to say goodbye, and tears threatened at the very thought of parting. But, at least, he was almost back to normal health, she consoled herself, and a few more days should see him moving around the house, or even a gentle stroll to the bodega to investigate the progress of the wine-making.

Later that evening, she was surprised to find Luis waiting for her in the dining-room. Of late, they had rarely been together over dinner—Luis arriving afterwards, or leaving as she was about to sit down—and tonight it seemed strange that he had waited.

'Sorry, are you expecting guests?' she asked politely, hesitating in the doorway.

'No, Serena. It's just the two of us,' he replied, drawing back a chair. 'We need to talk.'

She waited, a little bewildered by his welcome and reluctant to join him at the table, knowing that any conversation with him was bound to lead to harsh words. But he advanced towards her, the expression in his eyes curiously appealing as he reached for her hand.

'Please, Serena,' he coaxed. 'This is the first evening I have been able to relax since the harvest began.' And he drew her to the chair, ensuring she was comfortably seated before he went round the table to seat himself opposite.

This evening, she noticed he had taken more than usual care with his grooming; his dark hair was smoothed back but still inclined to curl just above the collar of the immaculate silk shirt he wore. And, as he had shown her to her chair she had caught a hint of expensive cologne, the same as he had worn on that first night in Barcelona.

Suddenly aware of his close regard, she said a trifle coolly, 'Well Luis, what was it you wanted to say?'

He drew a short breath and leaned back in his chair, his eyes never leaving her face. 'First,' he began, 'I meant what I said earlier about the care you have given Senor Miguel. I'm not sure if you are aware that I look in on him a number of times each day, and the change I saw in him each morning was unbelievable. Secondly, Doctor Ferrer was right, Serena—you knew what was needed, and I can't thank you enough.'

'Thank you, but it is what I trained for,' she reminded him with a casual lift of her shoulders.

'I think you are being extremely modest, Serena, and if you were to reproach me about my doubting remarks concerning your qualifications, then I rightly deserve it,' he admitted with a rueful smile.

Serena returned his smile, even though she was slightly apprehensive about his generous apology. 'I prefer we forget all about it,' she offered, 'as I don't want there to be any animosity between us when the time comes for me to leave.'

'Must you leave?' he asked, his eyes searching her face as he reached for the wine bottle. 'Senor Miguel is going to miss you.'

'I know, but I must go,' she replied firmly, knowing it would be so easy to weaken, 'though I would like to visit again, early next year. That is, if you don't object?'

Luis shrugged expressively. 'Why should I object when you have given him a new lease of life?' he pointed out and reached across the table to cover her hand, adding softly, 'I also prefer we remain good friends.'

She glanced up, suddenly nervous under his close scrutiny. His amiable manner bewildered her and she simply nodded and eased her hand away. Luis then went on to further amaze her by suggesting she needed a break and, now the vineyard made less demands on him, there was still time for her to do a little sight-seeing with him in his car.

'Senor Miguel will not be alone,' he assured her. 'Marie-Sofia is arriving tomorrow so he will have company which will give you a little more time to yourself.'

'But I have not minded the time I have spent with him,' she objected, but broke off as

Rosa brought in their meal.

'I know,' he continued quietly. 'But, until recently, you have worked day and night and now you deserve a rest. We will discuss it further tomorrow but for now, let us enjoy our meal.'

Rosa had excelled herself this evening, presenting them with a local dish of roast duck and mushrooms served in a bitter chocolate sauce. And the Catalan cream with its brittle caramel topping, which followed, added further to Serena's pleasure. It was as though Rosa had prepared something extra special almost as a celebration, and, when Luis opened a bottle of champagne to go with the dessert, Serena found her spirits lifting. Perhaps it would be a pleasant experience to go sight-seeing with Luis. After all, in his present mood there was something rather special about him, too.

CHAPTER S1X

Serena awoke with pleasant memories of the previous evening filtering into her mind. Luis had kept her talking until quite late, engaging her in a discussion about local culture. Any tension between them had seemed to disappear.

And now, although she was unhappy over the thought of leaving, she was glad her relationship with Luis had improved and they would part company on friendly terms. She smiled to herself as she threw back the bedcover, her spirits high; even Genaro now made polite conversation with her during his visits to his grandfather, his solemn little face breaking into a smile each time she made an error in her Spanish grammar, or mispronounced words.

Luis wasn't at breakfast and it crossed her mind he may have regretted his more friendly attitude towards her the evening before. However, he did join her later to help Senor Miguel down the stairs. It was the third time her grandfather had ventured down and, this morning, he insisted on descending the stairs unaided, one hand on the bannister rail and a walking stick in the other, stating that he intended to visit the bodega to check the progress of the wine.

The cheer that went up when Senor Miguel arrived at the bodega brought tears to Serena's eyes, and a bottle of wine laid down in a vintage year was brought out to celebrate the occasion of his recovery. In the cool and musty atmosphere of the cellar, the cellar-master uncorked the wine with an extravagant gesture and, after some discussion, which Serena found difficult to follow, the wine was poured. But it was quite a while before a glass was handed to Senor Miguel, who held it up to the light, then rotated the glass to release its aroma. 'Excellent!' he exclaimed proudly, and those who had waited expectantly for his verdict smiled as he put the glass to his lips.

'I had begun to think I would never go back to the bodega,' Senor Miguel admitted as they returned to the house. 'But now I shall work again.'

Serena could see he was tired, and Luis had to help him into a chair in a shady end of the patio. It was oppressively hot today, she had noticed, which could mean her grandfather's forecast of a storm might prove correct.

'Thanks be to God the picking is finished,' Luis commented as they drank the coffee Rosa had brought out to them. 'A really heavy storm can do untold damage to the fruit, but now the must is flowing from the press I think I can relax.'

'I was hoping to gather some grapes myself,' Serena remarked a little disappointedly, 'but

I'm too late.'

'Perhaps next year,' Senor Miguel put in hopefully and, turning to Luis, he suggested, 'Why don't you drive Serena into the country, Luis? It would be small compensation for all that she has missed, and when Marie-Sofia arrives today I shall not be alone.'

'Exactly what I said at dinner last night,' Luis agreed as he relaxed in his chair, his long legs stretched out before him.

'Unfortunately, there's little time left,' Serena pointed out. 'In fact, I ought to ring the hospital in case my letter doesn't reach them in time.'

'Serena, must you talk of leaving?' Senor Miguel complained and, when she didn't reply, he drew Luis into his appeal.

'Well?' Luis queried, one eyebrow raised. 'Have you decided?'

'I'm afraid I must,' she said, avoiding to look in her grandfather's direction.

'Then we shall go for a drive tomorrow,' Luis decided. 'We will take the day off and drive into the mountains.'

Serena smiled in agreement but, as Luis continued speaking about the journey, she felt suddenly nervous at the thought of spending time alone with him. Luis was such a complex character she feared a whole day in his company could prove a disaster.

'How about an early start?' Luis proposed. 'That is, if the weather holds out.' And, glancing at his watch in dismay, he jumped to his feet to exclaim, 'I must leave you now— Marie-Sofia's train is due in twenty-five minutes!'

'I expect she will be exhausted after her journey,' Serena remarked as Luis drove away. 'It's so hot.'

Senor Miguel chuckled. 'I've never known her suffer, any ill-effects,' he confided. 'She's just like her father, full of vitality. You will see what I mean when you meet her.'

*   *   *

To say that Marie-Sofia was full of vitality was an under-statement Serena discovered when, little over an hour later, the visitor arrived. Luis's big black car drew up in a cloud of dust and, when he came round to open the passenger door, a slim young woman alighted and threw her arms round his neck. 'Here at last!' Serena heard her exclaim delightedly as she clung to the smiling Luis and, to her shame, Serena experienced a twinge of resentment over the closeness of their embrace.

When Marie-Sofia released him, she turned to wave to Senor Miguel. 'Papa, Papa, I'm here!' she cried excitedly and rushed on to the patio to kiss the older man on both cheeks. Then, turning to Serena, she offered her hand, saying, 'So you are the skeleton in Papa's cupboard. How do you do?'

Serena found the newcomer quite overwhelming but managed to murmur a suitable greeting. To be referred to as the skeleton in her grandfather's cupboard was hardly something she took kindly to, nor had she expected the visitor to be someone only a few years older than herself. And, as Marie-Sofia chattered on in rapid Spanish, too quick to follow, Serena let her attention wander to Tomas, who was busily unloading two cases of sherry and a large travelling bag from the boot of Luis's car.

'Ah, Serena!' she heard the woman suddenly exclaim. 'Forgive me, I should speak in, English.'

'I can understand if you don't speak too quickly,' Serena smiled, 'but please don't worry on my account.'

Marie-Sofia's red lips parted in a sparkling smile and she returned her attention to Luis. 'Why not come back with me, Luis, and take a holiday in Jerez? You look so worn out.'

Serena noticed that Luis didn't immediately take her up on her offer, but merely smiled and said, 'We have been very busy here, though I do intend taking a day off tomorrow.'

'Ah, then we can spend a day in the city,' Marie-Sofia suggested, her beautiful, dark eyes turned on Luis.

'I need you here,' Senor Miguel interjected—surprisingly quickly, Serena

90

thought. 'It will give Serena an opportunity to see a little of the countryside now I have you for company.'

Marie-Sofia merely shrugged, but Serena felt most uncomfortable. It had been her grandfather who had intervened but, she noticed, Luis hadn't objected to Marie-Sofia going along. She would catch Luis alone and offer to stay behind instead of Marie-Sofia. But, later, when the opportunity arose, Luis brushed aside her offer and informed her— 'I'll be ready to leave around eight-thirty, see you at breakfast,' before he went off to his study to work.

By the time she retired, Serena felt quite worn out. Marie-Sofia's chatter, combined with the meaningful looks she exchanged with Luis when referring to something in the past, caused her to feel knotted up inside. She reminded herself it was only natural exuberance on Marie-Sofia's part, considering she had not visited since earlier in the year. But, even so, a picture of the glamorous woman from Jerez clinging to Luis' arm was the last thing she saw in her mind before falling asleep.

The sun was streaming into the room from between the slats of the shutters when Serena woke the following morning. The night had been extremely hot, preventing restful sleep until the early hours when her thoughts had dwelt on Luis.

Downstairs, she found Luis and Genaro having breakfast and felt a small surge of relief at not finding Marie-Sofia already there. Genaro looked especially pleased with himself and reached over to pour Serena's coffee as she took her seat at the long, wooden table.

'No lessons today,' the boy announced happily, 'so I shall look after Grandfather.'

'Will you remind him to take his tablets?' Serena asked, smiling at the child's enthusiasm. 'He should take two after lunch, but I expect to be back before the next are due.'

'I thought we may have dinner somewhere, so don't plan to be back too early,' Luis put in, adding confidently, 'Genaro will make sure he has all his tablets. Don't worry.'

'Good!' Genaro cried delightedly. 'I shall be a male nurse—Serena has told me about them.' And he shot off his chair towards the door, pausing suddenly to ask, 'May I be excused?'

'Of course,' Luis smiled indulgently and, when the boy had disappeared, commented pleasantly, 'It seems you two are friends now.'

'I found him only too willing to help once we got to know each other,' Serena agreed. 'And he helps me with my Spanish.'

'A woman's influence may be good for my son,' Luis remarked, his eyes narrowing thoughtfully as he regarded her across the table.

'Perhaps,' she murmured and, folding her napkin, said, 'I'll just go up and say good-bye to Grandfather.'

'I don't see nurse anywhere,' Serena remarked ten minutes later as she walked with Luis to his car.

'I expect she is gossiping with Rosa in the kitchen,' he told her as he held open the passenger door. 'Though I must admit she is more efficient than before.'

'Even so, I hope Grandfather never requires her services again,' Serena said, as Luis slid into the driving seat.

'Should that be the case, we would have no alternative but to send for you,' he declared, regarding her with a hint of mockery as he turned the key in the ignition.

Serena felt he was laughing at her and, for some time as they drove along, she could think of nothing suitable to say. Finally, she managed a strained, 'Where are you taking me?' when she saw they had turned off the main road leading to the city.

Luis smiled. 'I was beginning to think you had taken a vow of silence,' he said, casting her a sideways glance. 'Actually, I thought you may like a ride over the mountains. The view is wonderful and you will see more of the area from there.'

'Do you mean the monastery I saw when I first came here?' she asked with increased interest. 'I'd love to see it.'

'Then you shall, but I intend taking you further than that. I planned to have dinner in a mountain restaurant . . . that is, assuming you would prefer somewhere that serves traditional food?'

'Definitely!' she agreed, her reserve melting now the atmosphere had become more relaxed between them.

As they drew near to the impressive natural beauty of Montserrat, she looked up at the great peaks in awe, experiencing a strange fascination for the closely-locked towers of rock, partly cloaked in mist. As the car began its climb, the powerful engine took the steep gradient with ease, and it was only when she looked out of the side window, down to the foot of the mountain, that she realised how far they had climbed.

'Nervous?' Luis enquired, giving her a momentary glance as they continued on their winding upward journey.

'A little,' she confessed, 'but it's a wonderful view.'

'Wait until you reach the monastery.' He smiled, selecting a lower gear. 'It is even better up there. The summit is well over a thousand metres above sea level.'

Serena couldn't conceal her small sigh of relief when they reached the monastery and Luis parked the car. They then went to take a look inside the Basilica, Luis guiding her through the crowds of visitors mingling in the square. Once inside, they walked in quiet procession at the rear of a visiting group, and when their turn came to view the carved image of the Lady of Montserrat with the child Jesus on her lap, Serena was fascinated.

'La Moreneta, the people affectionately name her,' Luis whispered as she gazed at the serene figure, delicately carved, and marvelled at the perfect condition of the embossed gold and silver surrounding it.

Outside, in the bright sunlight, she gazed around and exclaimed, 'It's beautiful! I never imagined all this was up here, or realised it's a working monastery.'

'And, don't forget, there's also the Escolania, the school for the boys' choir. An impressive number of past choir-masters received their training here, under the guidance of the Benedictine monks,' Luis told her as they wandered past the cloisters, its stone arches guarded by a tall cypress tree. 'The choir sings daily, but I'm afraid we are too early for that,' he added as he led her over to a low wall on the other side of the plateau. 'Perhaps another time.'

A trifle nervous of what she would find, Serena hesitated a moment before looking over the wall to the vast area below. Luis noticed her slight hesitation and came to stand behind her, his warm hands resting on her upper arm, providing her with a sense of security as she took in the breathtaking scene.

'Oh, Luis, what a splendid view!' she gasped, and felt his fingers tighten a little on her arms.

He smiled at her delight and, after a few moments more, suggested they move on. And, it was on their way back to his car that she spotted a record on display in one of the shops, the sleeve showing a picture of the Montserrat boys' choir. 'An ideal memento of your visit,' he said and drew some notes from his pocket.

Serena thanked him and, taking the slim package from the assistant, added, 'I shall enjoy listening to this when I'm back home.'

With a flicker of a smile, Luis turned away and sauntered back to the car park and, as they drove away, taking the steep turns in low gear, he kept his attention on the road. Serena had enjoyed the experience immensely but, she wondered, how did Luis feel? Would he have preferred the woman from Jerez to be by his side?

As they left the pinnacles of rock behind them, Luis opened the sun-roof to allow a breath of air to enter the hot interior. Serena welcomed it and, about to comment, she glanced at Luis to find he appeared to be deep in thought. Was he inwardly yearning for the company of Marie-Sofia? Was this outing merely a duty he felt bound to perform because her grandfather had suggested it? Perhaps his own offer had been made out of politeness in the hope she wouldn't accept.

Tormented by these thoughts, she experienced a pang of guilt when Luis asked, 'You look very serious, Serena. Are you not enjoying yourself?'

'Yes, of course,' she managed quickly. 'The scenery is so beautiful. I'm glad you brought me here.'

'So many people think Spain is nothing but crowded beaches, and pseudo-English bars. They never see all this,' he commented, gesturing through the window as they drove along the dusty road of a quiet village, its white-washed houses slumbering in the sun.

'I must confess I hadn't realised it would be quite so scenic,' she agreed. 'It doesn't do to have preconceived ideas about anything.'

'Or anyone,' she thought she heard Luis murmur as they left the village behind.

Shortly, Luis pulled the car off the road, suggesting they take a walk before going on to the next village for lunch. Serena was glad of Luis' guiding hand as they wandered over the stony ground where goats grazed on the rough, dry grass and the scent of aromatic herbs drifted on the heavy, warm air. And when, on level ground, he didn't release her hand, she felt an unexpected tremor of pleasure and glanced up to catch his smile.

Exhilarated by the exercise, she was eager for the refreshment he proposed and, in the next village, she waited in the car while he enquired about a meal. As he chatted to the proprietor of the restaurant she couldn't help but admire his casual yet immaculate appearance; his finely knitted grey cotton shirt and matching tailored slacks enhancing his dark looks and lean, muscular frame. And when he turned, smiling as he beckoned her from the car, her heart gave a tiny, unaccountable lurch.

Lunch proved to be a lengthy meal taken in the cool atmosphere of a room where palm trees stood motionless outside the window, and the window-box was ablaze with colour. The food was delicious; a perfectly cooked variety of local produce served to them by the family.

'This is a perfect time to relax, away from the heat of the day,' Luis remarked as he filled her glass with cool spring water.

'It's very pleasant here.' She smiled contentedly, her earlier turmoil forgotten now that conversation was easy between them.

'I want this day to be a pleasant memory for both of us,' he said, reaching across the table to squeeze her hand.

Managing a wavering little smile, she felt a sense of relief when he went on to tell her his plans for the remainder of the day. They would drive on to Montseny, exploring the villages on the way, then dine in some mountain restaurant and drive back home by motorway.

Serena found it to be a fascinating excursion when, in the first village, they watched the skills of a man in a small ceramics factory as he drew tiles of traditional design from an antiquated kiln. And, in the last, they rested on a seat in a shady square under the leafy umbrella of the plane trees with their prettily mottled trunks.

'Is there anything else you would like to see?' Luis asked, as they left the square to stroll along the narrow streets. 'The shops are opening for the evening now.'

'I want to buy a small present for Genaro,' she said. In a small shop, she bought him a colourful story book, and also some chocolate for her grandfather.

As they left the shop, he pointed to the mountain beyond the buildings. 'That is where we are going,' he said, smiling at her obvious amazement. But, after travelling only a few kilometres of rough uphill road, he glanced up at the sky, observing a little anxiously, 'Clouds are beginning to gather to the west. Perhaps we should turn back and dine somewhere else.'

'Oh, how disappointing after we have come this far,' Serena sighed. 'I would have thought it much too sunny for rain.'

'One can never tell,' he said gravely. 'Here, storms can appear with very little warning and these roads can be treacherous.'

'Then it is up to you, Luis,' she said, hoping to hide the disappointment she felt. 'You're the driver.'

Luis glanced sideways and smiled. 'I hate to disappoint you, Serena, so let's risk it. Your grandfather would consider me totally irresponsible,' he continued, his lips twitching humorously. 'He did say a storm was brewing.'

'Then you must blame me, Luis. It could be ages before this opportunity comes my way again.' And she gave a smile of satisfaction as the car increased its speed.

Way up the mountain, the road became deeply rutted and narrow and she could hardly believe the restaurant Luis had spoken of existed along such a wild track. It was growing dark when the first sign of the village came into view, a scattering of old houses partly hidden amongst the trees. Driving slowly between them, Luis searched for the hotel which had been recommended to him. And, when they did find it, standing alone in a clearing with the Catalan flag of four bold red stripes on a golden yellow background mounted above the door, it appeared almost deserted.

'How's this for a taste of local culture?' Luis asked laughingly as they walked into the hotel and entered a small room where a group of men chattered noisily at the bar. 'I don't suppose you expected anything quite so rustic.'

'It's charming!' Serena enthused.

Luis shot her a smile as the proprietor good-humouredly bustled two young children out of the bar so that he could take their order. 'They are curious to know who is here with the big black car,' Luis translated as a hush fell over the room.

'No wonder! We must be the only strangers here,' she replied, aware of the interested glances in their direction, though the talking resumed once their curiosity was satisfied.

Luis nodded. 'Which is why they don't bother with a printed menu,' he explained. 'I'll enquire what is available.'

Serena had difficulty trying to imagine the local dishes Luis described and it was a great surprise when the proprietor's wife took her firmly by the hand and led her into the kitchen. In the spotless, tiled cooking area, the woman lifted the lids off the pans to show her what they contained and gave a lively account of their ingredients. The mouth-watering aroma rising from one particular dish caught Serena's interest, so she pointed to it before going back to join Luis in the bar.

'That is the first time I've made my choice in the kitchen!' she exclaimed laughingly. 'Though I'm not sure what it is.'

'It's probably the rabbit cooked with almonds,' he said when she described the dish. 'It's a speciality of the house. I've ordered xato to start, which is a type of salad with anchovies.'

Eventually, in the small dining area, they sat down at a table covered with a white tablecloth. 'I never thought I could be so hungry,' Serena remarked, as she tucked in to pieces of rough, toasted bread rubbed with garlic and spread with tomato and olive oil. But they had hardly started on the xato when a distant rumble came from outside and a cheer went up in the bar.

'Thunder, I suspect,' Luis commented. 'Everyone sounds delighted at the prospect of rain.'

'Perhaps it is only in the distance,' Serena offered hopefully, but Luis shook his head and peered out through the small window.

'There is not a star in sight,' he reported. 'In fact, it was dark earlier than usual tonight.'

'Would you prefer to leave now?' she asked when a second rumble sounded, louder than before.

'No, Serena. I don't want to spoil your day, we can leave after our main course and have dessert and coffee somewhere else on the way. Once we are off the mountain, travelling will be easier.'

Apologising for her rather selfish desire to come this far, Serena started on her main course which was served in a hot earthenware dish.

'Don't blame yourself. I was just as eager to come here,' he assured her, his smile returning. But Serena almost dropped her fork when a tremendous crash of thunder struck almost overhead, following a streak of lightning that lit up the road outside.

The thunder and lightning continued, and then the rain started. She had seen nothing like it before, streaming in torrents down the windows, hammering so heavily she feared the glass would break.

'We may as well have dessert here,' Luis suggested. 'We would be soaked to the skin if we tried to reach the car.'

Serena chose fruit as her dessert and accepted a small liqueur with her coffee, though she had noticed Luis took only a little wine in consideration of the drive back. And, eventually, the sound of thunder faded into the distance and the rain ceased its heavy pounding on the window. Serena went to look outside, but the scene that met her eyes caused her to gasp in dismay, bringing Luis to her side. In the dim light from the windows of the hotel, she saw a stream of muddy water coursing along the narrow road, taking with it debris of broken branches and stones.

'If may not be quite so deep once we reach the fork in the road lower down,' he told her, 'but, if we don't get moving soon, we could find some of the rock face has become dislodged.'

Holding an umbrella over them, the proprietor led the way to the car. Luis had taken off his shoes and rolled up his slacks before he picked Serena up effortlessly in his arms. Setting her down on the driving seat, he waited for her to slide over before getting in himself and retrieving his shoes from the proprietor, who remained staunchly in position until the door was closed.

'That was kind of him,' she commented as they began to move slowly forward down the road to the sound of muddy water churning under the wheels.

'Particularly kind, considering it is the first time I have been here,' Luis agreed, peering closely through the windscreen. 'Actually, he offered us a bed for the night but I thought we should make an attempt to get back.'

'Oh,' Serena said softly, experiencing a brief but inexplicable longing to be stranded with Luis. But, she wondered, was his urge to get back in any way connected with Marie-Sofia? During the pleasant evening she had almost forgotten the glamorous woman from Jerez. 'Yes, we should get back,' she found herself agreeing crisply. 'I shouldn't have persuaded you to come this far.'

'Serena,' he reproached in a quiet voice. 'Don't spoil it.'

Confused by his response, she remained silent as he selected a lower gear to meet the fresh surge of water pouring in from the rocky roadside. She heard him mutter a soft oath, and she gripped the rich upholstery of her seat, when, in the beam of the headlights, she saw huge pieces of rock fall in to the road ahead. Cursing under his breath, Luis brought the car to a sudden halt and stepped out. But he had hardly left the car when she heard his sharp exclamation as a splatter of stones fell around them and a huge mass of mud and rock slid down on to the road in front, cutting off any further progress they hoped to make.

Leaping back into the driving seat, he quickly found reverse gear and drove carefully back up the hazardous track. 'We had better get out of here before any more comes down,' she heard him say, and she had never felt more helpless in her life. She was used to emergencies of an entirely different kind; now she could do nothing but sit there, hoping he could escape the danger in time. She ached from tension as the car slithered and shuddered back up the dark and tortuous road.

A short distance on, he stopped and let out a long, rasping breath. 'I think we are away from the worst of it,' he announced. 'Somewhere near here, there is a gateway. I should be able to turn the car there.'

'Is this the only way down?' she gasped in alarm, and when he nodded she closed her eyes in dismay.

'Don't be frightened,' he said softly, reaching for her hand. 'We will go back to the village and take rooms in the hotel. It would be madness to risk any of these mountain roads tonight, especially now, when the rain has started again.'

Serena opened her eyes to see huge drops of rain bouncing off the windscreen and knew there was no alternative but to do as he advised. She had every confidence in his ability and knew, with Luis beside her, she was perfectly safe.

When they finally reached the hotel, the building was in darkness. This time, Luis parked the car on slightly higher ground near the entrance and knocked loudly on the heavy, wooden door. Soon they heard the sound of bolts being withdrawn and the proprietor opened the door, one hand cupped round the flame of a candle to protect it from the draught.

'The road down is impassable,' Luis told him as they were beckoned indoors. 'There has been a rockfall only two or three kilometres away. I would like to take you up on your offer and stay here overnight.'

'I did wonder how you had fared,' the proprietor said as he led the way to the bar and placed the candle on the table between them. 'If you will wait here one moment, I will ask my wife to make up the beds.'

'It is quite common for the electricity to be cut off during a storm,' Luis told her, as the proprietor moved off in the direction of the kitchen. 'But I expect they will have plenty of candles in stock.'

'I like it.' Serena smiled. 'It's sort of— romantic.'

'Romantic!' Luis echoed, a twinkle of humour lighting his eyes. 'I'm glad you are taking it so well, Serena. Not that there is anything I can do.' He spread his hands expressively. 'But at least we will have shelter and a bed.'

'We could telephone—assuming there is a phone here,' she suggested. 'Genaro and Grandfather are sure to worry.'

'Obviously, you didn't understand the owner when he told me there are no lights or telephones working in the village,' Luis explained. 'Most likely, the lines are down in this area only, so they will have heard the news on the radio. Don't worry, they will know we are safe somewhere.' He smiled confidently. 'In the meantime, I propose we have a bottle of his best cava wine, as it is unlikely I'll be driving tonight.'

When the owner rejoined them, he was clutching a bottle in one hand and two tall glasses in the other. Handing them over to Luis, he then appeared to be indicating the way they should take to reach their rooms and, lighting a second candle, he showed them to the foot of a flight of bare stone steps.

'Senor, senora,' he said with a slight inclination of his head as he bid them goodnight and stood aside to allow them to pass.

'I assume there are more candles in the rooms,' Serena whispered as she held the flickering light high so that Luis could negotiate the steps.

Luis didn't reply but quietly nudged open the first door on the landing and held it while she took the light inside.

'Is this my room, or yours?' she asked in a low voice as Luis came to place the bottle and glasses on the bedside table.

'We can discuss that over a drink,' he replied softly as he tore the foil from the top of the bottle and released the wire holding the cork.

CHAPTER SEVEN

Having grown more accustomed to the dim light, Serena looked around, her eyes travelling up to the low, beamed ceiling and down to the solid mahogany wardrobe standing against the far wall. She saw two single beds with striped cotton covers thrown over them; old fashioned, but suited to the room.

The soft hiss as Luis eased out the cork interrupted her visual exploration. 'For you,' he said, offering her a glass of the bubbling liquid. And, as she took it from him, he clinked his against it, saying, 'To us,' and, as his gaze lingered upon her, added, 'and the night.'

'Mmm, lovely!' she murmured appreciatively as the drink went down. 'This should help us relax.' And, laughingly, she warned, 'I hope your room is close by—you may get a little tipsy.'

A smile began to form on Luis's lips. 'Much closer than you have realised obviously,' he said softly, still holding her in close regard as he refilled her glass.

'Closer than I realised . . .' she began blankly, her eyes widening suddenly as realisation dawned. 'Not here!' she gasped. 'You're not intending to sleep here?'

'It is the only room free, Serena. We have

no choice.'

'B-but this is a hotel,' she spluttered. 'It must have more rooms!'

'Ah, but only a small hotel,' he pointed out with a casual lift of his shoulders. 'The owner's mother is staying, also his sister who kindly vacated this room and moved in with her children.'

Serena shook her head in exasperation. 'But didn't you tell him we're not married?' she cried, just as a thought struck her. The proprietor had called her 'Senora'—had he presumed them to be man and wife?

'It appears he does think we are married. Still, at least your reputation will be safe,' he mocked. 'Quite frankly, I have no intention of sleeping in the car.'

Wordlessly, Serena met his defiant stare. Obviously, he wasn't in the mood to be argued with and, as he came towards her, she held out her glass. Perhaps another glassful would numb her nerves. To be confined in this room for a whole night with a man as attractive as Luis filled her with a certain feeling of trepidation.

But, instead of filling her glass, Luis slid his arm round her waist, saying cajolingly, 'Come on, Serena. Don't go silent on me again. There is no alternative—we've got to stay here.'

The appeal in Luis's eyes was almost too much for her and, before she could check herself, she shot back, 'Then it is a pity

Marie-Sofia isn't here instead of me!' And she struggled from his grasp.

'But I'm with *you*, Serena!' he hissed, reaching for her again.

'Not by choice, I shouldn't think!' she retaliated, brushing past him. But she had barely taken a step away from him before his hand shot out to curl round her wrist, bringing her back to face him. And, before she could begin to object, he had cupped her chin in one firm hand as his head came down to capture her lips in a forceful kiss.

At first, she struggled against him, but she was no match for his powerful embrace. 'Don't fight me, Serena,' he coaxed softly, releasing her lips for a moment to gaze down on her.

There was something about his gentle entreaty that made her cease her struggles, and when his lips came down for the second time they were less demanding, teasing hers apart. The exquisite sensation they evoked was something she couldn't fight and she became pliable in his arms. Then, with a quickening heartbeat, she responded to his kisses, her hands sliding up around his neck and he drew her even closer.

Serena was unaware of anything else at that moment. Even the distant roll of thunder didn't penetrate the cloak of pleasure in which she was wrapped. It was Luis who slowly drew away, a smile flickering round his mouth as she looked up at him with dazed eyes.

'What's wrong?' she murmured huskily, trying to focus on him through the haze of pleasure.

'Nothing, cara,' he whispered, his lips warm against her forehead. 'It is just the sound of thunder.'

'Does that mean the storm is returning?' she asked, mentally shaking herself back to earth.

'Maybe. But it will not trouble us here, Serena, you are quite safe with me.'

'Mmm.' She sighed contentedly, snuggling against him, 'I'm so glad you're here,' she said, and looked up into his eyes, her expression soft and tempting.

Luis's arms tightened around her as he sought her eager lips. Shivers of pleasure rippled through her as the heat radiating from him penetrated her thin cotton dress, and his lips grew more insistent as his caressing fingers pressed her against his lean body.

Again, it was Luis who drew back, speaking her name in a voice that was husky with passion. He closed his eyes and let out a long, wavering breath, fighting the yearning within him.

'Damn you, Serena,' he groaned through clenched teeth. 'You are so desirable I find it hard to resist you.' And, thrusting her away from him, he picked up the bottle and refilled their glasses.

The atmosphere of the room seemed to grow cool and Serena shivered as she struggled to gain control over her shattered emotions. 'It—it's this ridiculous situation,' she stammered, clenching her fists as she searched for words. 'I should never have agreed to stay.'

'Why did I have to be stranded here with you?' he continued as if she hadn't spoken, his voice tinged with aggression.

'Would you have preferred Marie-Sofia?' she threw back in angry humiliation. 'I'm sure she would have been delighted!'

Suddenly, there was a half-smile on Luis's face as he advanced towards her, forcing her back to the edge of the bed. His hand shot out, the long fingers lifting her chin so that she had to look at him. 'Serena, you are jealous!' he exclaimed with an amused stare, his eyes glittering in the candlelight. 'You are jealous of Marie-Sofia.'

'Don't be ridiculous!' she cried, jerking her head away to escape his mocking, dark gaze. 'Why should I be jealous of her?'

'Because, my dear Serena,' he began with lazy arrogance, releasing her chin as he towered above her. 'Although you may deny it, I think you are in love with me.'

With her head still averted, she gave a savage gasp of indignation. 'Never!' she flared. 'You'd be the last man I'd choose—you're despicable!'

At this, his expression changed. 'Then you have no need to worry, Serena. I would never force my attentions on an unwilling partner.'

He turned away from her then, leaving her to cope with the turmoil of her emotions as he went round to the other bed. From behind her came the rustle of clothing and the creak of the mattress and she knew he had gone to bed.

She stole a glance across to the other bed and, in the low flickering light, saw he was lying with his back turned in her direction, the smooth, tanned skin of his shoulders contrasting with the brilliant whiteness of the sheet drawn up to his waist. She stared at him for a moment, trying to convince herself she didn't care. It had been foolish to bring Marie-Sofia into the conversation and she strongly regretted ever mentioning the woman's name. Luis was right—she was jealous. And, even though she tried to put it from her mind, the feeling persisted in troubling her. Stifling a sob of frustration, she tore her eyes away from him and looked towards the window. Through the heavy lace curtain she caught the occasional flash of lightning as the thunder continued to rumble in the distance and, without bothering to undress, she pulled the bed-cover over her head to shut out the storm. She knew she was in love with Luis; there was no other way to account for the feelings he evoked within her, both mind and body.

For a few moments, Serena wasn't aware of what had awakened her until a brilliant flash of light lit up the whole room. And when the next roll of thunder crashed overhead she cried out in sheer terror, convinced the building was being torn apart. She also wasn't aware of Luis sliding out of his bed until he was beside her. He whispered, 'Don't be frightened. I'm here.' It was strangely comforting, in the dark.

'Oh, Luis!' she gasped, tensing as the storm continued to rage. 'For a moment I didn't know what was happening.'

'It is only a storm, you're quite safe,' he murmured soothingly, his arm going round her shoulders to draw her closer.

Relief flooded through her as she felt the security of his embrace.

In the next flash of light she caught the glint from his eyes as he looked down on her, and he smiled as he gathered her more tightly in his arms.

Luis was no longer in the room when she opened her eyes to find the sun streaming in through the lace curtains, but the sound of running water was coming from the bathroom where, she assumed, he was taking a shower.

It wasn't long before he came out of the bathroom, looking almost as immaculate as he had the day before. Only the dark shadow around his chin told of his unexpected overnight stay, and his manner was pleasant, but cool.

'I thought it better to let you sleep on,' he said, as she swung her legs to the floor. 'I'm going to have a look at the condition of the roads but I'll order breakfast for you on the way out.'

Serena murmured something about the state of her dress as she smoothed down the skirt but found it difficult to be quite normal with memories of the night still clear in her mind.

Serena sighed and went into the quaintly antiquated bathroom where she took an almost cold shower. But it was some time before Luis came back, his clothing splattered with mud.

'The local men have been working since daybreak, he reported, 'so I felt obliged to lend a hand.' And he went off to wash the mud from his hands before sitting down to breakfast.

As they drove down the mountain, along the narrow track which had been cleared only that morning, Luis appeared quite cheerful, though not inclined to make conversation, whereas Serena's spirits were low. And Luis's comment on the heaps of mud and rock at the roadside where they had come to a sudden halt the previous night did nothing to ease the tension she felt. But she waited to speak to him about it, knowing he needed to concentrate until they got off the mountain road.

Once off the mountain, though even this had not escaped the ravages of the storm, she glanced across at him with a tentative, 'Luis?' before she went on to say quietly, 'I would like you to know I was grateful for your thoughtfulness last night.'

'To what do you refer?' he queried with a brief glance in her direction. 'Is it the few words of comfort I gave?'

'I mean the storm, of course, though I suppose I should be grateful that you didn't take advantage of me,' she concluded coolly.

'You are a very desirable young woman, Serena, but I would have been a fool to allow my feelings to run wild with you.'

'What ever do you mean?' she gasped angrily.

He gave her a bitter smile. 'Really, Serena, I'm quite sure you are aware that a woman in your position could manipulate the situation to her own advantage. I'll admit I was tempted, but I have yet to be convinced you are on the level.'

'On the level . . .' she began furiously, but she was so angry, words failed her and she quickly averted her head to stare unseeingly through the side window.

'Yes, Serena, I have to be sure. You must have realised I viewed your coming here with some suspicion . . .'

'You made that very plain,' she interjected coldly.

'But now I feel quite an affection for you,' he continued more gently, as if she hadn't spoken, 'and I would like you to stay until this matter has been dealt with.'

117

'Stay!' she cried as her head spun round in his direction. 'You want me to stay here?'

'Yes—or, at least wait a little longer . . .'

'No, Luis,' she hissed. 'I am leaving the day after tomorrow, and as long as you are around it can't come soon enough!'

*   *   *

Serena was grateful no-one was around when she and Luis returned to the villa. She went immediately to her room and stayed there until late afternoon but, by evening, she knew she would have to conceal her unhappiness at her argument with Luis, and visit her grandfather. She excused her late appearance by saying she was tired, the storm having kept her awake, and did her best to convey to him her pleasure over the outing, when all the time her heart was aching and her pride was shaken apart. And, even though the old man made no comment, she suspected he sensed something was wrong and she was grateful to escape the scrutiny of his eyes when he suggested she have an early night.

But, into the early hours, Luis continued to dominate her thoughts, making the need to succeed at her coming interview even greater—a busy working life would lessen the agony she now felt.

The following morning she waited in her room until she was sure Luis would have left the house. She had just reached the head of the stairs when Rosa's voice came from the hall below to tell her she was needed on the telephone. Picking up the receiver, she recognised the hospital manager's voice on the line. Her letter had arrived only this morning, the speaker told her, adding that he had recommended her for the post, and would like her to come for an interview.

'I'll be there,' Serena assured him. 'I was getting a little anxious, so I'm grateful you rang, and I will telephone you immediately I get back.'

Replacing the receiver, she turned to go into the dining-room just as a shadow fell across the hall, and her heart gave a sickening jolt. Luis ushered her into his study and closed the door, leaning against it so that it was impossible for her to escape.

'You can't keep on avoiding me,' he growled. 'So stop behaving like a child.'

'You're the one who's being childish,' she returned. 'What do you hope to gain by bringing me in here?'

Disregarding her remark, he went on to ask, 'May I know who that was on the telephone?'

'It was a private call,' she reminded him with all the dignity she could muster. 'If you must know—'

'Was it Mortimer?' he interrupted with obvious anger.

Feeling that Luis deserved all he got, she

merely smiled and observed the muscles of his jaw grow tense.

'So it was!' he grated, his dark eyes boring into her as he demanded, 'What in hell's name does he want with you?'

'Actually, he's asked me to marry him,' she announced, and a hint of triumph lit her expression as she saw Luis's fury increase.

'Impossible!' he thundered, coming to bring his fist down on the polished desk. 'You are not leaving here!'

'Oh, yes, I am!' she retorted with a defiant lift of her chin. 'Don't forget, my ticket expires tomorrow. I may as well use it—I'd hate to be dependent on you for my fare!'

Luis didn't try to prevent her leaving as she flounced past him, her emotions nearing breaking point as she flew back up the stairs. The fact that she had salvaged some of her pride by telling him it was Clive on the phone did nothing to compensate for the unhappiness she felt.

Brushing away her tears, she composed herself sufficiently to go to her grandfather's room to break the news of her departure. She found him reading a newspaper out on the terrace, and he looked up and smiled as she joined him. 'You're looking extremely well this morning, Grandfather,' she greeted him, stooping to bestow a kiss on his cheek.

'Actually, I feel like going to work in the bodega but Ferrer won't allow it.' The old man smiled. 'What about you? Are you going into the city with Luis?'

Seating herself beside him, she felt a lump rise in her throat. 'No,' she managed eventually, 'we have nothing planned. I wanted to spend the day with you. I must leave tomorrow, on the early flight.'

'So soon?' she heard him ask, a catch in his voice.

'Yes, I'm sorry. I've had a wonderful holiday and you have been very kind . . .'

'Kind!' he repeated, in an incredulous tone. 'Dios, child, I owe it to you.'

'You don't owe me anything,' she told him gently. 'I was delighted to be able to help restore you back to health.'

He shook his head. 'No, I was not thinking of that, this is a debt I have yet to repay,' he said and, raising his arm to gesture in a wide arc over the land before them, continued, 'Your mother, your grandmother, they should have shared this with me. But it is not too late, Serena—you shall be amply provided for.'

'Grandfather, I don't want anything,' she protested. 'It is not why I came—Genaro, and Luis, they are your family.'

He smiled and assured her, 'I have already ensured Genaro's future is secure, and Luis has ample security of his own.' He paused a moment before going on to explain, 'I have had time to think about the responsibilities I had cast aside for all those years and they have

121

troubled me. So now you are here, I can compensate a little for something I should have done a long time ago.'

'Grandfather, you must not blame yourself. Circumstances were very different then. If my grandmother's parents opposed your being together there was nothing you could do.'

'But you shall not suffer, Serena, I shall send for my solicitor—'

'No!' Serena cried. 'I have security of my own,' she lied, 'so please don't do anything like that.'

'Then why must you return on account of this promotion you spoke of?' he asked, casting her a shrewd glance. 'I thought you liked being here.'

'I do, and I'm delighted we have come together at last,' she told him truthfully. 'It is just what I have to do. But I shall visit you whenever I have leave,' she promised as she rose, dropping a swift kiss on his forehead before she left.

Although Serena wanted to spend most of her remaining time with her grandfather she found it hard to cope with his pleas for her to stay. But how could she explain the situation between her and Luis, or the reason for their conflict? Her grandfather had a high regard for his son-in-law and the last thing she wanted to do was cause a rift between them. Unable to settle, she dragged her suitcase from the wardrobe and flung it on the bed. Perhaps if she started her packing, it would be a more positive way of facing what was now inevitable. About to start sorting through her wardrobe, she hesitated on hearing a tap on her bedroom door. For a moment she held her breath, fearing to answer it in case it should be Luis standing there. There was a second tap before the door slowly opened and Marie-Sofia's dark head came into view.

'Ah, you are here!' Marie-Sofia exclaimed in a pleased voice. 'I am missing you today.'

'I thought it was time I started my packing,' Serena explained. 'I didn't want to leave it until the last day.'

'So you have not changed your mind, Serena,' she said coming into the room. 'Senor Miguel was hoping you would.'

'I know, and I feel dreadful about it,' Serena confessed. 'But I do intend to come back next year.'

'For a man of his years, that is a long time to wait,' Marie-Sofia pointed out. 'He looks so well at the moment. I hope your departure doesn't mean he'll regress.'

'Please, don't remind me,' Serena implored, and to her dismay she felt a tear coursing down her cheek.

'Ah, tears!' the Spanish woman exclaimed, her expression filled with concern as she came to place her arm around Serena's shoulders. 'Tell me, Serena, are they for your grandfather, or Luis?'

123

Serena's head jerked up. 'Luis?' she cried. 'Good grief, Marie-Sofia, whatever gave you that idea? You're more likely to shed tears over him than I.'

Marie-Sofia gave a knowing little smile. 'I think you love him, that's why. I have noticed the way your eyes follow him, and the way he looks at you . . .'

'Simply your imagination,' Serena said a trifle shortly as she shrugged the woman's arm away. 'I wouldn't waste tears over him if he was the last man on earth! No, he's all yours, Marie-Sofia, and you're welcome to him.'

'Serena!' the woman exclaimed protestingly. 'Luis and I are merely good friends, and have been for years . . .'

'Please,' Serena intervened stiffly, 'I don't wish to know.'

'But I can't allow you to leave feeling so unhappy about Luis. I know how a woman feels—you must believe me,' Marie-Sofia appealed and, on a more thoughtful note, continued, 'Luis is a kind and generous man who never thinks only of himself.'

'Never?' Serena queried with a trace of scorn. 'I doubt it.'

'No, never,' Marie-Sofia reiterated. 'And even his recent problems haven't changed him. He is still a thoughtful man.'

'Problems of his own making, I should think,' Serena put in rather acidly but, glancing at her visitor's face, saw a flash of anger in her expression.

'Then why did you instruct your solicitor to act the way he did?' Marie-Sofia flared. 'What do you think that did to Luis?'

'I—instruct my solicitor?' Serena gasped in amazement. 'I don't know what you mean.'

'I mean the solicitor who telephoned this house after you received Senor Miguel's first letter,' the raven-haired woman prompted, her dark eyes fixed on Serena's face.

'First letter?' she queried blankly, meeting Marie-Sofia's cool stare. 'I only ever received one.'

'I refer to the first one, the letter Senor Miguel had his solicitor send to you before he divulged any details of your existence to Luis,' Marie-Sofia told her and hesitated a moment, waiting for Serena's reaction before she continued. 'But it was Luis who directed him to send a second letter, insisting you visit, because Senor Miguel was too ill to do it himself. He couldn't bear to see the old man so upset because you hadn't replied.'

'But I only received one letter,' Serena insisted, 'please believe me, Marie-Sofia. And it must have been the second one as it mentioned Grandfather's illness.'

'Then how do you account for the telephone call which came less than two weeks after the first letter was sent?'

'I can't . . . I have never even spoken to a solicitor since Mother died almost a year ago,'

Serena protested. 'And I don't understand why you connect it with me.'

'If you knew what the solicitor said to Luis, you would understand!' the other exclaimed rather savagely. 'Though, of course, he never mentioned it to Senor Miguel.'

'Then tell me,' Serena begged helplessly. 'For Heaven's sake, tell me!'

For a moment, the other woman appeared uncertain, her dark gaze assessing Serena's helpless appeal. 'Very well,' she conceded finally, 'now we realise you are not here merely to gain, I will tell you.'

'We?' Serena queried bitterly. 'You may have realised it but I doubt if Luis has changed his opinion.'

'No, no, you are wrong!' Marie-Sofia cried, coming to rest her scarlet-tipped fingers on Serena's arm. 'Naturally, he was suspicious at first and expected you would try to inveigle yourself into his and Senor Miguel's favour, but you would not have cared for your grandfather so well when it was only by his death that you stood to gain.'

'To gain from anyone here was the last thing on my mind,' Serena assured her, 'but you still haven't told me what the solicitor said.'

'Ah, yes, the solicitor—or so he professed to be,' Marie-Sofia added, with a curl of her crimson lips, before she went on. 'He said he was acting as your financial advisor, though it was obvious to Luis he was hoping to gain an estimate of Senor Miguel's wealth. Of course, the man didn't put it quite so bluntly but he did mention that you couldn't afford the fare here and he would ensure any financial help Senor Miguel was willing to offer would go directly to your account.'

Marie-Sofia paused and shook her head. 'Thank God it was Luis who answered the telephone, or Senor Miguel may have fallen foul of this man's deception. And Luis didn't enlighten him, even though the speaker claimed to be acting on behalf of your mother's dependants.'

'On behalf of Mother's dependants?' Serena echoed, her expression one of blank amazement. 'I don't understand . . .'

'And that is not all,' Marie-Sofia continued, 'Luis continued to allow the caller to think he was speaking to Senor Miguel, particularly when he asked if your grandfather's relatives were aware you existed, if indeed any remained and, should the family honour be at stake, both he and you, Serena, could be persuaded to be most discreet.' Marie-Sofia hesitated, a gleam of triumph lighting her dark eyes as she laughingly went on—'But Luis was clever. Still speaking as Senor Miguel, he pleaded poverty, his business in debt, and suggested that you, Serena, as a relative would feel it your duty to help him.'

'I can't believe it!' Serena gasped as the colour drained from her face. 'I never employed a solicitor—and why would anyone telephone on the pretext of it being on my behalf? Apart from the hospital, no-one knows I have a relative here—' She broke off suddenly as a thought struck her. 'Clive . . .' she whispered shakily as she sank down on the bed. 'It must have been . . .'

'Serena! You look very pale—are you all right?' Marie-Sofia's concerned voice penetrated Serena's numbed mind. 'I'll call Luis.'

'No, please don't,' Serena begged, forcing herself to respond. 'I'll be fine. It's just a headache, perhaps you will tell him I'm resting.'

'Of course. But please don't mention anything about what I have just told you.'

'I won't,' Serena assured her and, even after the Spanish woman had left, she remained seated on the bed thinking over all Marie-Sofia had said. What had happened to her grandfather's first letter? Clive had dealt with all legal and business mail concerning her mother, but why hadn't he mentioned this particular letter to her? It had only been because Clive was away that she had opened what she now knew to be the second letter, addressed to both Mrs and Miss Ferguson, asking her to come here. Reflecting on his interest in her ageing relative, she was convinced Clive was the culprit and, as she considered more carefully all Marie-Sofia had told her, it was becoming increasingly clear to her why Clive hadn't shown her the first letter or kept his appointment with her in Barcelona. Clive must have assumed from that first invitation that her grandfather was a wealthy man, but when Luis had given him a totally different impression over the telephone he had ceased to be interested.

Uttering an angry sigh, Serena rose and moved over to the window. It was humiliating to think that Clive had only wanted her for the money he had hoped she would inherit, and it was obvious to her now, once Luis had convinced him otherwise, he had persuaded her to come to Barcelona with no intention of joining her, simply to get her out of the way and out of his life.

Yes, she knew she was right, and as soon as she got back to England she wouldn't hesitate to challenge him about the matter, particularly the telephone call which almost amounted to blackmail and, quite clearly, had put a smear on her character in Luis's eyes. She stifled a groan. She had told Luis she intended to marry Clive. What would he think of her now?

It was almost as if by thinking of Luis she had brought him to her door when there came a firm knock and he requested to come in. Evidently he had disregarded her pretence of a headache.

From the open doorway, Luis silently surveyed the room, from the gaping wardrobe doors to the suitcase lying on the bed. 'What is it, Luis?' she asked, avoiding his eyes. 'I'm rather busy.'

'So, you still intend to leave in the morning, yes?' he demanded to know, his stance faintly intimidating.

She lifted her head in a defiant gesture. 'You know I must.'

'Even if I ask you to stay?' he asked and, when she simply nodded, he gave a hiss of exasperation. 'Then, to save you future heartbreak, perhaps you should see this,' he directed coldly, drawing her attention to the glossy magazine he was holding. And, thrusting the open pages before her eyes, he read aloud—'Society speculates on the future of the daughter of one of Madrid's wealthiest families and her current escort, a London businessman.'

Wordlessly, Serena stood there as the print swam before her eyes. 'Added to that,' she heard Luis continue, 'there is a report in today's paper of him being arrested for fraud. I'm sorry, Serena, but I had to make you aware of what a scoundrel Clive is. I also warned the family in Madrid.'

'It doesn't make any difference,' she cried brokenly. 'Whatever you say, I'm leaving,' and she flung herself away from him, unaware of the anguish in his eyes as she raced down the stairs.

It took Serena a while to calm down after

that but, as she made her way along the orchard path, she realised it wasn't the fact Clive had deceived her, but the fact that Luis had drawn her attention to it that had made it difficult for her to conceal her distress. She was in love with Luis, but she could never agree to stay, knowing he had no similar affection for her. And the very thought of having to spend another night in this house and face him at dinner was more than she could bear. There was a chance there would be a seat on the late afternoon flight for that day and, with luck, she could escape the house without coming face to face with Luis again.

Luckily, when she finally got through to the airport, she was able to secure a seat on the afternoon flight. Next, she found the number of a taxi company and arranged for them to pick her up at half-past two. She knew it would mean a long wait at the airport but she dare not risk leaving it any later, in case Luis confronted her again.

To Serena's dismay, as she put down the receiver, she turned to find Marie-Sofia standing in the dining-room doorway. 'I've had to change my plans,' Serena explained in a shaky little voice. 'I will be leaving this afternoon.'

'I already overheard,' Marie-Sofia admitted and with a shrug of resignation, she said, 'It is unlikely Luis will be back in time. He's gone to Barcelona.'

131

'I don't think he will be too concerned, Marie-Sofia. But I had better go up and tell Grandfather.'

*   *   *

Putting the last few items in to her case, Serena checked her bag for her passport and flight ticket. She sighed as she picked up the handbag—this had been the start of it all, she recalled miserably. If it hadn't been for this bag Luis would never have known Clive had not kept his appointment with her. If . . . She frowned. It was pointless going over it all again. She reached to the top shelf of her wardrobe to take down her pink straw hat. Standing in front of the mirror, she placed the hat on her head, knowing the time had come to say goodbye to her Grandfather, Genaro and Marie-Sofia . . . but not Luis.

Forcing a brave smile, Serena waved her hand until the small group of sad-faced people standing on the villa steps were out of sight. And, as the taxi sped away in the direction of the airport, she silently brushed away a tear. As she had hoped, Luis hadn't arrived back by the time the taxi had called but now she felt an ache of misery at the thought of not seeing him again.

Deep in thought, it did not seem very long to Serena before the bright facade of the airport building came into view. She alighted and paid the driver and, as he unloaded her luggage, her eyes wandered to the distant mountains set against a sunny backcloth of brilliant blue.

Inside the bustling airport hall she went towards the row of check-in desks, picking out the one which dealt with her flight. She noticed the London flight was still high on the departure board but she chose to join the long queue for the desk knowing her wait would be more comfortable without the added weight of her case.

With her boarding card tucked safely in her bag, she glanced at her watch and decided to look around the shops and take some refreshment in the main hall to help pass the time. Eventually, she came to the book stall where she browsed through the tourist guides, finally choosing one about Barcelona to occupy herself during the flight. But, as she ran her eyes over the news-stands, one picture in particular seemed to stand out as though to challenge her. It was a mountain scene with the words 'After The Storm' printed beneath. Quickly averting her gaze, she moved back into the main hall, pausing to watch a fascinating water fountain on her way to the refreshment area.

Seated at one of the tables, she ordered a cool drink and, deep in thought, looked idly around as she waited to be served. 'Senorita?' she heard and, startled by the intrusion into her thoughts, looked up to find the waiter with her order just as a lone tear escaped to run down her cheek. Seeing his concern, she forced a quick smile and glanced away. But the memories from that night on the mountain, together with all Marie-Sofia had told her, refused to fade, adding to the conflict in her mind.

Suddenly becoming aware of the passing time, she finished her drink and hurried along the vast hall towards passport control, noticing her flight was due to be called. But, as she slowed to withdraw her passport from her bag, she felt certain she heard her name called over the speaker system. She hesitated when the announcement came again, 'Will Senorita Serena Ferguson go to the information desk.'

Anxiously looking around in search of the information desk, Serena was unprepared for the jolt to her senses. There, striding purposefully towards her, was Luis, his unsmiling expression changing to one of relief as he drew near.

'I heard the announcment . . .' she began as he reached her side. 'Is something wrong?'

'Yes,' he replied tersely, as he propelled her away from the entrance to passport control.

'Is it Grandfather?' she asked worriedly, quickening her pace to keep up with his long stride. But Luis didn't reply until they were outside the airport building, though his expression told her this was something serious.

'No,' he replied finally when they had almost reached his car, hurriedly parked at the end of the building.

'Is it Genaro?' she queried with an expression of concern as he opened the passenger door and indicated for her to get in.

'I will tell you on the way,' was all he said as he strode round the car and slid into the driving seat and, without another word, put the car into gear and accelerated away.

Driving only a short distance from the airport, he suddenly pulled off the busy main road and brought the car to a standstill under the shade of the pine trees.

'But—the announcement! I thought you said it was urgent!' Serena gasped in alarm. 'I'll miss my plane!'

'Yes, you will,' he agreed shortly and, turning in his seat, he took her by the shoulders as he yelled, 'Why did you try to leave before I returned?'

'Is that the only reason you brought me here?' she cried angrily. And with rising panic, she insisted, 'Take me back to the airport immediately. My luggage is already checked in.'

'Damn your luggage!' he said, 'I need you here.' And, pulling her roughly towards him, he captured her lips with cruel insistence, conveying to her the frustration of his mood.

Her mind reeling, Serena struggled in vain against the hard contours of his chest as his lips continued their relentless invasion of her mouth. And, when he finally drew away, there was a kind of savage satisfaction in his expression as she very audibly caught her breath.

Somewhat bewildered, she gave a faintly derisive laugh. 'You need me!' she exclaimed mockingly. 'I don't think so, Luis.' But the slight quiver of her lower lip betrayed her and she saw a hint of tenderness enter his smile.

'Believe me, Serena, I do,' he murmured. 'I realised it the moment I reached the villa and you weren't there.'

'Oh, Luis,' she whispered in a choked little voice, tears threatening to start at any moment, 'please, don't hurt me again.'

'I won't, querida,' he promised gently as he retrieved her hat from where it had fallen behind the seat. 'I was a fool not to trust you.'

'Was?' she queried. 'Have you now changed your opinion of me?'

'Serena, I wanted to trust you, and I will admit I tried to provoke you to test your sincerity,' he confessed with a rueful smile. 'But you continued to devote yourself to Senor Miguel despite my unforgivable behaviour.'

'I never received that first letter, the one Grandfather sent before he was ill,' she told him quietly. 'I would have replied had I seen it.'

'You know about that?' He gave a sigh of regret and said—'I should have asked you about it before, instead of allowing my suspicions to override my instincts.'

'You made it very difficult for me,' she reminded him with a bitter smile. 'But I'm glad we've cleared the air between us.'

'I know,' he agreed remorsefully. 'And it took the shock of not finding you at home this afternoon to bring me to my senses.'

'I should never have allowed you to believe it was Mortimer who telephoned me,' she offered contritely, letting her hand remain in his. 'It was bound to make you mistrust me.'

To her surprise, Luis chuckled. 'No, my darling—when I questioned Rosa afterwards I discovered the call was from a London hospital, though I must confess I was furious at the time. The very idea of Mortimer ever holding you in his arms nearly drove me wild and I gave vent to my frustration by being very rude—until I remembered . . .'

'So you experience the odd twinge of jealousy, too,' she broke in to remind him, her heart giving a tiny, but strangely pleasant, jolt. But, seeing his thoughtful expression, queried—'What was it you remembered?'

'Where you are concerned, yes, I am jealous,' he affirmed. 'But, when I recalled the night I came to your room in Barcelona, when you thought I was Mortimer and announced you had changed your mind about him, I knew then that you would not willingly become involved in a casual affair. And, that night on the mountain, I wanted you, desperately, but I didn't want to take things further until we had the opportunity to discuss Mortimer and the letter—which I intended we should do this evening.'

'Oh, Luis, why did you leave it so late?' she asked. 'I wish you had told me before. He means nothing to me now.'

Luis shrugged. 'My fault entirely, Serena, but I thought you despised me.' Then, to silence her protest, he added quickly, 'I wouldn't have given you up that easily. I intended to make one more appeal to you tonight.' He paused as the sound of jet engines came from overhead and, glancing at his watch, remarked, 'That will be your plane, I should think.' Thoughtfully turning her hat in his hands, he said, 'Thank God you were wearing this, otherwise I may never have seen you in time.'

Serena smiled as he tossed the hat into the back seat and, drawing her towards him, he kissed her mouth again, this time very softly. Her heart seemed to miss a beat and a sensuous shudder ran through her as he gathered her close to him. She was totally unaware of all around her then; the click of grasshoppers basking in the warm sun, and the hum of distant traffic coming through the open car window went unheeded as she yielded her lips to the gently increasing demands of his. Lifting his head, he took a steadying breath to

138

ask, 'Will you come back to the villa with me, Serena?'

'For how long?' she asked, on a trembling note. 'I should telephone the hospital.'

'For ever,' he broke in huskily, tilting her chin so that she was compelled to look up into his dark, smouldering eyes. 'I'm asking you to be my wife, Serena. Will you marry me?'

'Oh, Luis,' she sighed. 'We've not known each other for very long.'

'Long enough for me to know I love you, querida,' he murmured, raising her hand to his lips. 'I love you so very much.'

'Then I will,' she agreed softly. 'That is, providing we can have our honeymoon somewhere in the mountains.'

'Where better?' he smiled. 'I will telephone the hotel immediately we are home!'